HER BABY SECRET

HER BABY SECRET

BY

KIM LAWRENCE

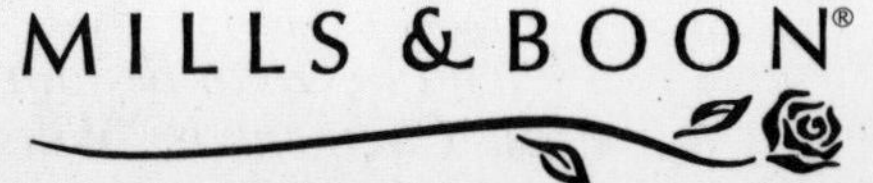

First published in Great Britain 2002
Large Print edition 2002
Harlequin Mills & Boon Limited,
Eton House, 18-24 Paradise Road,
Richmond, Surrey TW9 1SR

ISBN 0 263 17353 4

Set in Times Roman 16½ on 17½ pt.
16-0902-53981

Printed and bound in Great Britain
by Antony Rowe Ltd, Chippenham, Wiltshire

CHAPTER ONE

QUINN, his lean body clad in supple motorcycle leathers, strode into the swish foyer of the world-famous magazine *Chic*.

The glass swing doors closed behind him and, green eyes narrowed, he paused for a moment to get his bearings. Nothing in his attitude hinted at the fact that he knew that had the person he sought known he was there he would undoubtedly have found himself chucked out on his ear!

By nature Quinn was a confident individual—in his experience assurance was far more likely to open doors than an apologetic manner—but he considered this situation called for a extra degree of audacity. The meek might well be going to inherit the earth but Quinn couldn't wait that long—he was a man with a mission!

At any time Quinn had the sort of face that made people look, and then look again, their eyes admiringly drawn to the pleasing arrangement of strong bones and intriguing manly hollows that made his irregular features stand out from the crowd. At that moment his expression—a fairly accurate reflection of his one overriding emotion, *determination*—drew more second glances than usual.

His steely purpose extended beyond the tight-jawed, edgy expression on his saturnine features, his entire lean, loose-limbed body was tense with resolve; even his soft-footed tread had something uncompromising about it. In fact Quinn oozed danger, and human nature—or at least *female* nature—being what it was, this was the fatal ingredient that had every woman in the place instantly riveted.

In the normal run of things Quinn wasn't much bothered about the impression he made on people, except when, as part of his professional role, he needed to put them at their ease. His present enterprise was purely personal, and he had other, more urgent, things on his mind than racing pulses! He was going to see Rowena, and if that involved an unseemly contretemps with a security guard, chaining himself to an immovable object or just generally making a spectacle of himself, so be it!

Dignity had its place—hell, he was great at dignity, he oozed the stuff morning till night—but now wasn't the occasion to display restraint. He'd been displaying it for the past couple of months and where had it got him…? Fobbed off, ignored and generally given the run around, that was where!

His chiselled jaw tightened another notch as he contemplated the abysmal way Rowena Parrish, his long-time friend and recent lover, had been treating him since that memorable night in New York.

No, the time had arrived for a little bit of positive action. Quinn wasn't a man accustomed to dealing with rejection or failure, and he was damned if he was going to accept it now without some sort of explanation. It would have to be an extremely good one too if it was going to satisfy him!

'I'm here to see Ms—' he began firmly as he approached the nearest of the receptionists arranged around a big half-moon-shaped desk.

'Oh, and she'll *definitely* be glad to see you.' There was a fervent nod of agreement that slid like a Mexican wave down the line of pretty faces.

It wasn't that the other applicants hadn't been good-looking. Like this one they'd all been sheathed in sexy black leather, and unlike this clean-shaven specimen they'd had the air of dissipated ruggedness that went with a sprinkling of designer stubble. Despite this advantage none had even come close to matching the indefinable something extra that this guy had by the bucketful!

The receptionist and her companions had all been watching his approach, mouths slightly ajar. His every physical attribute—these included legs that were longer than long, narrow hips, a washboard-flat belly and wide, powerful shoulders—had been digested, drooled over and stored for future dreamy reference.

Quinn, ready to do battle, was a little taken aback by this response. He cleared his throat and frowned suspiciously—was this some new devious ploy of Rowena's to get him out of her hair?

'Right, then, I'll just go to…?'

'If you'll give me your name I'll let them know you're on your way up.'

'Quinn Tyler.' There was no instant start of recognition—good, Rowena hadn't left any instructions to have him thrown out if he showed up as she had done at her apartment building.

After a lot of judicious eyelash fluttering the young woman consulted the screen in front of her. 'We haven't actually got you down…it must be some sort of mistake.' There were fervent nods of agreement. 'No problem, I'll just add your name here,' she told him cheerfully.

It was slowly dawning on Quinn that there was some sort of mistaken identity thing going on here, but as this seemed to be working in his favour he didn't see much point setting the record straight. If it got him closer to the inner sanctum and Rowena he was quite happy to play along, though that might be easier if he knew what role he was meant to be playing.

He dismissed any lingering qualms with a philosophical shrug—it couldn't be worse than a punch-up with Security, could it…?

Elbow leaning on the desk, he shamelessly utilised his most winning smile. 'That's very good of you…' he consulted the name badge pinned to her ample bosom '…Stephanie.'

A couple of minutes later, his fixed smile faded abruptly as he stepped into the glass-fronted lift and it began its smooth ascent. He looked at the piece of paper the nubile Stephanie had thrust into his hand, and his brows rose cynically at the sight of a scribbled phone number before he crushed it carelessly between his strong fingers.

The directions he'd received from Stephanie took him to a long, narrow room that contained a row of chairs and little else furniture-wise.

Quinn blinked; he was looking at a leather fetishist's dream. Males, mostly a few years younger than himself—mid to late twenties, he estimated—filled the available chairs. They were all clad in a similar fashion to himself—black leather from head to toe.

As he was surveying the surreal biker reunion scene in front of him, a door just to his left opened and he turned to see a short female figure dressed in a garish combination of lime green and cerise emerge, carrying a clipboard.

'Who's first?' The black leather rose *en masse* in response to her slightly bored query.

Apparently oblivious to the sudden rise in testosterone levels and anxiety, she ignored all the figures trying desperately hard to be rampantly male and turned instead to the one conveniently closest—ironically he was the only person present not trying to catch her attention.

'You! You'll do…' Her eyes travelled up the six-foot-five frame, getting wider and wider the more she saw. She paused, blinking in bemused fashion when she eventually encountered the greenest pair of eyes she'd ever seen. Long, curly ebony lashes any woman would have traded her soul for and equally dark, well-defined brows were suitable accessories for these truly spectacular orbs.

Sophie had seen it all but even she couldn't repress a tiny sigh of feminine appreciation.

He might not be trying, but this guy was succeeding fairly dramatically on the rampant male front!

Her eyes eagerly slid over the strong, hawkish nose that bisected the hunk's lean features and dropped to the wide firm line of a sensationally sexy mouth. A slow grin spread across her features.

'You'll do very well indeed,' she told him with a throaty chuckle.

Quinn, aware of a battery of resentful eyes on his back, found himself being bundled by the tiny figure through the door and into the connecting room.

In contrast to his colourful escort the elegant female behind the desk was clad totally in black. She looked at Quinn for a full thirty seconds before smiling—he had the distinct impression her facial muscles didn't get a whole lot of practice with this procedure.

She rose to her feet. 'Anna Semple.' Instead of extending her hand as Quinn had expected, she walked around him, head on one side in a bird-like attitude—he found himself thinking 'vulture' at this point. 'And who might you be?' Anna asked, somewhat taken aback to discover that, instead of looking eager to please, this candidate was glancing at his wrist-watch.

'Quinn Tyler.' He couldn't decide whether he was amused or irritated by the treatment.

'I haven't got a Quinn Tyler down here,' her colourful companion revealed, consulting her list.

'No matter.' His interrogator frowned as though his name was tugging at her memory. 'These don't look like props.' She ran a hand lightly over the sleeve of his well-worn leather jacket and gave another vulpine smile.

'They're not.'

'And have you done much of this sort of work, Quinn Tyler...?'

Time to ditch the subterfuge and move on to his main objective. 'Actually I think there's been some sort of...' He edged surreptitiously towards the door.

'Who sent you?'

'Nobody sent me.'

'Initiative! I like that, don't I, Sophie? But you have an agent?' If he didn't this opened all sorts of interesting possibilities—such as an exclusive contract. Now wouldn't that be nice? *Very* nice, she decided, trying and failing to discover any flaws in the hunk. Forget the leather spread—this guy could front their 'new season—new man' feature that was to run for three consecutive issues, she thought excitedly.

Quinn was a patient man, but even he had his limitations. He'd seen farmers giving prospective purchases at a livestock market a more subtle survey than this female was giving him! Any minute now he was convinced she'd ask him to show her his teeth! He was almost right…

'Take off your shirt and jacket, will you?' Anna requested, casually retaking her seat.

Quinn's eyes widened as it dawned on him she was deadly serious. And I thought *my* job called for personal sacrifices! he thought.

'Is that all?'

The younger woman looked startled by his response, but the irony sailed right over the older female's head.

'Yes, that'll be sufficient.'

Anna flicked her female companion an amused look as the big man remained immobile. 'Not shy, are you?' she taunted indulgently.

'Not shy, no,' Quinn replied honestly. Just a bit particular about who I take my clothes off for. The thought of removing his clothes focused his mind forcefully on his original objective—*Rowena*.

Now, if *she'd* asked him his response would have been quite different. With reluctance he dragged his mind clear of the various stimulating scenarios it had immediately conjured up along this theme.

He was just about to break the news that, whatever they had in mind, he wasn't available when the door behind him opened a crack, and the sound of voices drifted in—one at least he identified instantly.

'Have I got the go-ahead on the ''Having It All'' feature, Rowena?' Sylvia Morrow urgently hailed her editor who, oblivious to the admiring male eyes lining the wall, was taking a short cut through to her top floor office. She'd worked hard for that office.

Rowena was a tall, beautiful young woman with typical English-rose colouring, classical features, natural ash-blonde hair and a shapely but slender body. She was not unaware of the impact her looks made on people, but she felt on balance that these attributes had been more of a hindrance than a help in her single-minded efforts to gain the right to call that office on the top floor her own.

The job of editor that went with the luxury office was still new enough to seem unreal. It was the goal she'd been working towards ever since she'd left university with a first-class honours degree, no experience, no money and boundless ambition.

Now she was there—she had it all! Funny, she'd expected success to feel quite different. The route to the top hadn't been easy—people had said she was too young and some still were saying it—but she was proving them wrong.

The vague feeling of anticlimax was, she supposed, to be expected. Perhaps if her personal life wasn't such a mess she could have enjoyed her moment of glory, but ironically she'd never felt more confused or unhappy in her life. And whose fault was that? *Quinn Tyler's.*

She conveniently ignored the inescapable fact that she herself was at least fifty per cent to blame for her present predicament.

'Are you all right, Rowena?' Sylvia's concerned glance slipped from the haunted expression on her boss's pale face to the slim hand pressed against her enviably flat belly.

They had both been at the glitzy party of yet another new perfume launch the previous evening, the food and drink had flowed freely and Sylvia, who was congenitally incapable of refusing freebies, had woken feeling a trifle *delicate* that morning. It seemed unlikely Rowena had overindulged too—self-control was Rowena's middle name.

Rowena smiled stiffly and, trying not to draw attention to her action, removed her hand from her stomach. If she wasn't careful, she thought worriedly, people were going to start putting two and two together.

'I'm fine.' She was in control now and didn't show even by so much as a flicker of an eyelash the conflict that was raging in her head.

For someone who'd mouthed off as often as she had about how impossible it was for a woman to give her all to a job when she had a baby, this was some position to find herself in. Actually, it was some position for *anyone* to find themselves in! Not that she had a baby yet… She sighed, aware that she could fool others but not herself. No matter how hard she attempted to think of the new life inside her as a cluster of cells, she couldn't. It was a person—in the primitive stages maybe, but still a little individual.

'The "Having it All" feature…?' Sylvia prompted.

Rowena pushed aside her personal problems—for the first time in her professional career the process wasn't easy. 'You know my opinion on that one, Sylvia.' Rowena didn't believe you could 'have it all'.

Sylvia nodded. She did know; it was no secret that their dynamic new editor considered women who thought they could combine a high-powered career with marriage and a family were fooling themselves.

Something, Rowena was on the record as stating, had to suffer, and she for one was not prepared to accept compromise in any area of her life. As for nannies, why have a kid if you immediately farmed it out to someone else?

You had to hand it to Rowena, she wasn't too bothered about being politically correct. Privately Sylvia thought Rowena's horror of maternity and marriage might have something to do with the fact that her boss did everything so *perfectly*. She doubted if Rowena had ever muddled through or made do with second-best in her life—a life which appeared to be planned down to the last second. At least she wasn't daft or unrealistic enough to imagine a woman could carry on being so totally in control like that when she had a young family.

'Well, I have several high-flyers who don't share your opinion and a feature that's just begging to be written. It can't fail,' Sophie predicted in full sales-pitch mode. 'A behind-the-scenes peek into the homes and offices of the rich and famous with pictures of their dogs, kids and whatever...you know, the usual humanising influences...'

The notion of voluntarily exposing your own children to the media made Rowena grimace. Her gut response was extra strong no doubt because the whole motherhood issue had suddenly taken on a very personal aspect.

'It could work,' Sylvia insisted, sensing with dismay her boss's negative response.

'You're probably right, Sylvia.' With an effort Rowena focused her thoughts on the matter in hand. 'Who have you got lined up?' She was too professionally astute to allow her personal prejudices to get in the way of good copy.

'Maggie Allen.'

Rowena's delicately arched eyebrows rose. 'A topical choice.' Maggie Allen, the controversial new appointment to head an international pharmaceutical firm, was the sort of woman who genuinely did seem to have it all:

a loving, supportive husband, two well-adjusted children and her career.

How often, Rowena wondered cynically, did Maggie get to spend time with those children? And how long before the understanding husband started looking for a woman who could spend more than the odd hour or two with him?

'It gets better,' Sylvia enthused confidently over her shoulder. 'Hold on a tick, I just need to give Anna this layout.'

Rowena followed the resourceful writer through the door.

'Anna, could you—? *Oh, my god!*' Rowena heard Sylvia exclaim as she came to an abrupt halt.

Anna Semple saw her colleague's reaction and looked complacent. 'I rather think you can send the others home, Sophie. We've got our man.' She gave the tall figure who held centre stage a look of proprietorial approval.

It didn't take long to see what—or rather *who*—had robbed Sylvia of speech. Rowena got an impressive glimpse of broad, firmly muscled shoulders and a strong, supple back before she averted her eyes—beef cake wasn't really her cup of tea.

Besides, a quick glance had already revealed a spooky and unsettling similarity of build and colouring between Anna's hunky model and Quinn, and Rowena had problems enough without any more reminders.

They'd got the poor guy to show off his pecs. Rowena experienced a pang of sympathy, which was probably misplaced. For all she knew, the man was perfectly at ease with using his great body to promote his career, or maybe he was an exhibitionist who revelled in being drooled over?

She nodded briskly to the other women. 'I'll leave you to it. Three-thirty in my office…Sylvia…?' At that precise moment the tall figure turned his head.

It didn't occur to her for even one second to believe the proof of her eyes. She was just so obsessed she was hallucinating—it was the only possible explanation. Pale-faced, she stared transfixed at the hormonal hallucination before her.

The half-naked man, his green eyes narrowed slightly, smiled languidly, displaying a set of even, pearly white teeth.

The gasp that emerged from her lips was faint, but audible enough to attract curious glances from the other women present.

This was worse than hallucination—this was *real*! Only one man in the world could combine that much sneery contempt and sexual challenge in a smile!

If her legs had actually responded to her urgent mental commands she'd have obeyed her first cowardly instinct and fled the room. As it was she had to think of something to say that wouldn't excite unwanted speculation from the women she had to work with. Women whose respect she needed.

Why here, why now, why me…? Especially why me! She took a deep breath. It was no good moaning about it, it was happening and she'd have to deal with it.

Of course she'd known she'd have to see Quinn some time—she still hadn't worked out *when* precisely that some time might be, but she'd known she'd be psyched up for the experience. She'd have worked out in advance what all his arguments might be when she broke it to him, and she'd have a suitable reply for each one. But most importantly she'd have her own messy feelings sorted out by that point!

Her voice, hoarse and accusing, broke the strained silence that had fallen. 'What the hell are you doing here?' Way to go, Rowena! She could almost smell the rampant curiosity in the quiet room.

'This is Quinn Tyler, Rowena, our model for the—' Anna began.

Model! Rowena threw the older woman a look of withering disbelief. 'He is not a model!' she exclaimed, scurrying forward to gather up Quinn's discarded shirt and jacket from the floor where he had obviously dropped them. How could he stand there with all those women ogling him? He was nothing but a damned exhibitionist!

'What is he, then?'

'Yes, Rowena, what am I?' Quinn drawled.

Colour flooded Rowena's face as she met the malicious wide-eyed innocence in his mocking emerald stare. 'Don't tempt me!' she choked, wishing she could wipe that smug grin off his face.

'Actually, Anna,' she explained, trying a bit belatedly to re-establish some dignity, 'Quinn is a doctor.'

'He doesn't look like any doctor I've ever seen,' the older woman responded sceptically. Hands on her bony hips, she allowed her eyes to wander up and down Quinn's lean frame.

Rowena couldn't argue that point. 'He scrubs up *almost* respectable,' she snarled, experiencing an abrupt dignity meltdown the instant she looked at him again.

'Why, thank you, Rowena,' Quinn murmured provokingly.

'It wasn't meant to be a compliment. Let's face it, put Jack the Ripper in Armani and he'd most likely look respectable,' she announced dismissively—actually Quinn in Armani or anything else was almost impossible to dismiss or ignore! With a forced smile she turned to the other women. 'We went to university together.'

'Oh, an old boyfriend.'

'I object to the old,' Quinn complained with a hurt-little-boy look that had the other women grinning.

Nostrils flared, lips pinched tight, Rowena rounded angrily on a startled Sophie. '*Not* an old boyfriend!' she announced emphatically. She looked to Quinn for support—not surprisingly, none was forthcoming. 'We were part of a group,' she began to explain laboriously. 'A group of like-minded—'

Quinn's deep velvet drawl cut her off. 'A group of earnest, élitist snobs who liked to congratulate each other at frequent intervals on how brilliant, how cultured, how much better than everyone else we were. Many's the time we'd sit there contemplating our glittering futures.'

'Quinn!' Rowena exclaimed, shocked.

Quinn met her outraged glare, an amused glint of humour in his eyes—eyes which she knew could unexpectedly change from deep emerald to subtle aquamarine. 'You trying to tell me I'm wrong?'

Rowena's face softened. Her lips were half-way to forming a rueful smile before she realised she couldn't afford to relax around Quinn. 'No, you're not wrong,' she admitted with a sigh. 'We were unbearably pleased with ourselves.'

Quinn switched his attention to the three other women. 'In our defence I have to add that we were all very young, and most of us aren't quite so arrogant nowadays!'

'If that's a dig at me…' Rowena bristled, growing angrily pink.

A disturbing lopsided smile tugged at one corner of Quinn's mouth as he contemplated her stormy face. 'It wasn't.'

Rowena wasn't willing to be convinced. 'Talk about a classic case of the pot calling the kettle black,' she muttered truculently. Her colleagues, who had never heard their leader sound truculent, exchanged glances—and as for *pouting*…!

'And I don't know how you managed to weasel your way up here, but I've a good mind to call Security and have you thrown out!' He had the audacity, not to mention ill judgement, to grin. 'You think I'm joking, Quinn—just try me.'

'No, I don't think you're joking—that would require a sense of humour, not to mention an ability to laugh at yourself.'

All those weeks of deprivation she'd put him through—he could have strangled her! His darkened eyes travelled from the smooth curve of her neck to the soft outline of her wide, generous lips—or maybe kissing her would be more appropriate…? The muscles in his throat worked hard as he visualised sliding his tongue between her lush lips—she'd make that hoarse little whimper low in her throat, the one that drove him a little crazy.

Rowena's even white teeth came together with a jaw-aching crack. 'Shall we leave my inadequacies out of this for the moment?' Her eyes slid of their own volition to the expanse of silky dark skin and her sensitive stomach muscles tightened. 'For heaven's sake, Quinn, cover yourself up!' she pleaded hoarsely.

She wasn't sure which was the worse, coping with her own weak, lustful reaction to the distracting sight of Quinn's powerful torso or coping with the knowledge that the other women present were leching over his smooth olive flesh and sculpted muscles too.

She didn't pause to consider the consequences of her impulsive actions—around Quinn that happened to her a lot—the urgent need to shield him from their lascivious eyes was just too strong to resist.

Actually the three other women were no longer looking at Quinn at all; they were too fascinated by the sight of their cool, composed editor desperately pressing a crumpled white cotton shirt protectively against the dark, hair-roughened chest of the tall, gorgeous man.

'I suppose you think this is funny?' she hissed. The physical contact had been a big mistake! For starters, being this close she couldn't avoid breathing in the warm, male, distinctly Quinn scent of his body—it had a dizzy, addictive quality.

'I don't know how you got here, or why you're here…' she huffed, tears of angry frustration springing into her blue eyes as Quinn stood there totally impassive while she attempted to cover him up. She was struggling with all manner of insane urges, most of which involved plastering herself against him. 'I take that back; you obviously came here to humiliate me!' she accused wildly.

As if I need any help!

Quinn responded with a quirk of one dark brow and a cynical twist of his sensual lips.

'You know exactly why I'm here, Rowena.' Threat, promise and warning, his deep voice held all three.

She stood by helplessly, her insides quivering as he took the shirt from her shaky hands and in a fluid motion pulled it over his head. He slid it into place, tucking it into the narrow waistband of his trousers.

What was he trying to do to her? Those leather trousers left nothing whatever to the imagination; they showed off every inch of his long, powerful thighs. Rowena tried to avert her eyes, but the glint of dull silver caught her eye and held it.

It was the same silver engraved buckle he'd been wearing that night, the night that she had unclipped it with trembling fingers. He'd taken her hand and pressed it against…don't go there, Rowena! she warned herself frantically.

Too late! Erotic images complete with taste and touch and smell rose up in her head. His smoothly textured olive-toned skin covered in a fine layer of sweat…the raw rasp in his voice that had reduced her to a compliant, quivering heap of neediness…the unbelievable combination of triumph and tenderness on his face as he'd responded to her pleas and thrust powerfully up into her body, filling and stretching every part of her…

Hand pressed flat against her heaving bosom, she fought for breath, and a semblance of composure. The stabbing sexual desire that hit her was so tangible it was like walking into a solid wall of heat. She could feel the cold trickle of sweat as it slid damply down her back.

Quinn's slanted eyebrows quirked as he smoothed down the white fabric over his flat, leanly muscled midriff. 'Happy now?'

The action had mussed up his thick dark hair and without thinking Rowena reached up to smooth down his tousled locks. Her antagonism faded for a moment as her fingertips sank into his hair and brushed against his scalp.

She realised the implied intimacy of her thoughtless action at the same moment Quinn's head jerked back, the violent rejection making her lift her hurt eyes to his.

For a split second their glances collided before Quinn's heavy lids came downwards, veiling his expression. Rowena had seen enough in that moment's scorching contact to turn her insides hotly molten.

Their long-standing relationship had always been the sort where such innocent gestures were not misread. Well, news flash! Things had changed—big time!

But *when* had they started to change…?

CHAPTER TWO

AS SHE'D gone over the events in her head that had led to their becoming lovers Rowena had tried time after time to work it out, but she hadn't been able to pinpoint the exact moment that friendship had become something else.

It had begun before her short stint at the New York office, which the powers that be had deemed essential for someone about to take over the running of the London end of the operation. Rowena had needed an escort for a big charity bash and Quinn, who had just accepted a senior post at a major teaching hospital in the city, had stepped in at the last minute.

It wasn't as if she hadn't noticed, but after knowing him for so long Rowena took his spectacular looks for granted. The admiring glances he'd received that night, not to mention the envious comments she'd received from friends and acquaintances, had brought home to her just what a gorgeous creature he was.

It had been a good night—no, better than good—Quinn had a way of making his companion feel very special. He was also a great dancer, and an even better conversationalist—he had a dry wit and a clever tongue that had had her laughing half the night. She'd laughed so much that several acquaintances had commented on the fact, which had made Rowena wonder—for about two seconds—if she didn't take things a little too seriously as a rule.

'You were a big hit,' she told him when he dropped her off at her flat in the early hours. Head against the back-rest, she yawned and fished around for the shoes she'd slipped off her aching feet when she'd got into Quinn's Jaguar.

Quinn inclined his dark head. 'We aim to please.'

'So now I know how you manage to captivate all those women.' Quinn worked hard, but he played hard too. He had a taste for fast cars, motorbikes and beautiful women, but no staying power with the latter as far as Rowena could tell—not that she held this against him.

Perhaps like her he was married to his career, or maybe he hadn't met the right girl yet… The fleeting thought made her feel vaguely dissatisfied.

'If I didn't know you so well,' she teased him, adjusting the strap on her kitten-heeled sling-back, 'I might even make a pass at you myself.'

For what felt like a long time he looked at her, his expression enigmatic. 'Is that all that's stopping you?'

Rowena's smile didn't make it past the starting-post—there was no shadow of humour in his face, just a taut, dangerous expression that made the nerve endings deep inside her stomach tortuously flutter with excitement.

She couldn't remember what she'd said to fill the awkward lingering silence that had followed, but she knew his contribution had been nil. He'd just sat there and let her babble like an idiot.

One thing she did recall, very well indeed as it happened, was how it had felt when his arm had brushed against her breasts as he'd stretched over to open the car door for her. She had been mortified, not to mention confused, when her nipples had responded instantaneously to the brief contact. She had prayed he hadn't noticed them thrusting brazenly through the thin fabric of her bodice as she'd slid with a hastily mumbled thank-you from the car.

There had been no legitimate reason to refuse the series of invites that had followed—after all they were friends, and there was nothing wrong, she had told herself, with having a meal with a friend, or going to the theatre. As for walking by the river in the rain, what could be a more innocuous way to spend an evening?

Quinn's behaviour had given her no cause for complaint; there had been no repeat of that electric moment in the car. No, he had acted like the perfect gentleman despite the fact that she, for some perverse reason, had gone out of her way to recreate the moment—maybe it had been just to convince herself it had actually happened...?

Letting her hand linger longer than strictly necessary on his arm or knee, a lot more eye contact than was normal between them, making sure he'd been able to see her very excellent legs when she'd sat opposite him. Nothing *too* heavy or obvious; at least that was what she'd thought until one night, sitting in her flat after having been out for dinner, Quinn had bluntly demanded an explanation.

'I don't know what you mean,' she blustered. 'I'm not playing at anything.'

He dragged an unsteady hand through his thick hair. 'Well, whatever that *nothing* is you're doing, it's driving me crazy.' His green eyes came to rest on her face. '*You're* driving me crazy.'

'I am?' she exclaimed, unable to hide her pleasure. 'You'd never have known,' she added with a condemnatory frown.

After a startled moment Quinn began to laugh. It was such a warm, uninhibited sound she couldn't bring herself to be cross with him.

'Well, if you must know, I'm quite attracted to you,' she divulged bluntly. 'The idea takes some getting used to...' With a hint of bravado she raised her eyes and saw it was Quinn's turn to look pleased—and relief rushed through her. It would have been too embarrassing if she'd been reading the wrong messages.

'I think,' he replied huskily, 'that it might be worth the effort.'

Mesmerised by the stark hunger in his darkly lashed eyes, she felt her knees start to tremble. Her heart was battering against her ribcage like a sledgehammer.

He would be an excellent kisser—with a mouth like that how could he not be? she reasoned, allowing her gaze to rest dreamily on that stern, sensual outline. The idea of putting her theory to the test had her literally trembling with anticipation.

'You don't think it's too silly an idea, then,' she gasped, feeling a bit light-headed with relief—well, maybe relief wasn't solely responsible for that strange but marvellous floaty feeling.

Quinn took the wilful curve of her jaw in his hand, his fingers stroking the smooth skin of her throat. The touch was so gentle and his strength was so formidable that Rowena found the contrast deeply exciting. 'Not silly at all,' he replied.

His deep, husky voice sent tiny shivers up and down her spine. 'I knew you'd understand—you being not exactly big on the whole commitment thing.' Rowena was so relieved that she hardly registered the wary expression that flickered into his eyes. 'I mean, neither of us have the time to lavish on a *proper* relationship, do we?' she told him happily. 'With that whole pet name, flowers, and plans for the future stuff. Most of all the plans for the future,' she added with a heartfelt shudder. 'But we all have…needs.' It was probably ignoring hers that was responsible for her present distracted condition. 'I think I should be honest with you.'

'By all means be honest,' Quinn responded drily.

Rowena nodded, glad they were in accord. Quinn had let go of her chin and she wished he hadn't. She wondered if it would be quite acceptable for her to take the initiative and touch him…? God, but she wanted to, she thought, her eyes running covetously over his lean frame.

'Of course I've tried sex, but, I've got to admit, it wasn't an unqualified success. To be quite honest,' she added, the words coming in a rush, 'I'm terrible at it, but I'm willing to learn.'

She heard the stark sound of his inhalation and wished she'd not been quite so frank, but it was true: sexually she was what was popularly termed frigid. The first time might have been put down to inexperience, but the second time had been a full five years later, and though her lover—an attractive, experienced man she'd liked a lot—had been perfectly polite, she'd been able to tell he'd been in no hurry to repeat the experience, and actually neither had she. Since then she'd been able to channel her energies into her work—until Quinn.

'Let me get this straight—you want me for sex and nothing else.'

His low, very quiet tone sent a quiver of apprehension up her spine. Anxiously she searched his face but it was impossible to read anything from his enigmatic expression.

'Well, I wouldn't put it like that *exactly*.'

'Well, I would!' he yelled suddenly. 'I'd put it exactly like that. I've heard you called callous, Rowena. I've heard you called a cold, calculating bitch.'

Rowena flinched. It was a tired old sexist line that she'd heard many times before and it never failed to make her mad as hell—it hadn't hurt as it did hearing Quinn say it, though. It was nonsense, of course—a man who shared the qualities that made her good at what she did would have been universally admired for his skill, but not her. No, she was female so that automatically made her as hard as nails.

'And I've always stuck up for you, but I'm beginning to see how much you've changed since the old days!' he blazed. 'Sex isn't something you schedule like a finance meeting.'

Rowena listened to his diatribe in stunned silence. 'I didn't mean… I had no intention of insulting you, I just wanted to be upfront, Quinn.'

'I'm slow,' he reflected with a bitter smile, 'but not *that* slow. I don't need a diagram to tell me what you want.' At some level he was aware that he was overreacting—after all, he'd been propositioned before.

Quinn's scornful sneer reawakened her temper. 'I have to tell you, Quinn, I find all this righteous outrage at being treated like a sex object just a tad hypocritical coming from you of all people. I mean, a man with a track record like yours hardly screams commitment, does he? Or don't you like it when someone turns the table on you? The way you're going on anyone would think you wanted a serious relationship or something...' She saw his face and her eyes widened. 'Good god!' she gasped, horrified. 'You didn't, *did you*...?' She laughed in what was pure nervous disbelief, but he could hardly be expected to know that.

'I've been accused of being shallow in my time...' His voice had dropped to a soft, menacing whisper, but Rowena was in no mood to be intimidated.

'I can't imagine why,' she muttered belligerently.

The glacial flicker of his long-lashed eyes silenced her. 'But it would seem I'm an amateur compared to you.'

'The way I hear it you get by,' she retorted childishly.

'Then maybe you hear it wrong,' he cut back in a chilly voice. 'I may not be able to match your clinical objectivity, but I'm not totally unrealistic. I accept that some relationships are never going to go anywhere, but they're fun anyway. I've been there and done that, but not as often as you seem to think.'

Rowena hardly noticed this dry postscript; she was too busy dwelling on the lurid images drifting around in her head of Quinn *having fun*. She actually felt quite unwell—she'd had doubts about that lobster.

'Part of the excitement of entering a relationship is not knowing where it's going.'

Diverted by this peculiar viewpoint, Rowena forgot momentarily about the sick churning in her stomach. Personally Rowena always liked to know *exactly* where she was going.

'The exploration,' Quinn expanded forcibly. 'The wondering whether it might lead somewhere, whether she might be *the one*.'

Rowena's jaw dropped—it was something of a revelation to learn that Quinn believed there was such a thing as *the one*. Let alone discover he was actively looking for her. Boy, had she got Quinn wrong—the man was a *romantic*!

'With you there would be no wondering, we'd both know exactly where we were going—nowhere!' he continued.

Rowena's chin came up. She didn't much care for that combination of pity and contempt on his face. It was pretty obvious there was no point suggesting they went nowhere together.

'Let's call it crossed wires,' she suggested with an easy-come, easy-go shrug. Rowena had her pride and she didn't want him to guess how disappointed, mortified and frustrated she was by his rejection.

His own shrug was just as untroubled and dismissive.

Dragging her thoughts kicking and screaming back to the present, Rowena slid a wary, half-defiant look in the direction of her staff.

Their expressions were respectful enough *now* but Rowena wasn't fool enough to imagine that this situation would last for two seconds once she was out of the door. She hadn't gained her hard-nosed, cool-headed reputation by accident and now in two seconds flat she'd blown her cover wide open.

'*Happy?* Hardly,' she snapped venomously, fixing Quinn with a look of loathing. 'Well, if you'll excuse us, Quinn was just leaving.' Clinging to the tattered shreds of her dignity and trying to show she was still in charge, Rowena shoved Quinn's jacket at him and nodded imperiously in the direction of the door.

'So soon,' Quinn bemoaned sarcastically, throwing his jacket casually over his shoulder. 'We hadn't even started talking money yet.' He waved casually to the three watching women as Rowena, seething with exasperation, grabbed him by the arm.

'That would be right!' Rowena flared contemptuously—God, why couldn't she keep her mouth shut? 'You always did have your eye on the big bucks, Quinn. Why else go in for plastic surgery?'

'Perhaps I thought I could make a difference,' he suggested mildly.

Rowena sniffed, unwilling to admit even to herself that her accusation of avarice had been out of line, not to mention totally inaccurate.

Quinn was considered a world expert in facial reconstructive surgery and, though he did make big money from the high-profile clients who sought him out, Rowena knew he didn't restrict his expertise to those who could pay for it. The vast bulk of his workload was, and always had been, within the NHS, even though he could have made much more by working exclusively in the private sector. Not that money mattered to Quinn, coming as he did from a wealthy, privileged background.

'Three-thirty in my office, Sylvia!' Rowena called, putting a bold face on her unorthodox departure.

The three women exchanged glances as the door closed.

'I knew I recognised his name...' Anna cried. 'He did Lexie Lamont's new nose, so they say, and I saw him on that telly programme last month—the one about that teenager who got hit in the face by a jet ski.'

Sylvia nodded. 'I saw it; the girl got all choked up every time she talked about him.'

'Small wonder!' Anna exclaimed. 'Did you see the *before* picture? She mashed just about every bone in her face to pulp—all he had to go on when he rebuilt it were pictures.'

'There's no mistake, then, he's really a doctor. I suppose it's lucky we didn't send the others home,' her assistant reflected.

A naughty grin appeared on Sylvia's pretty face. 'Is it just me or do you get the impression boss lady isn't too keen on sharing...?'

The explosive sound of laughter was clearly audible to Rowena as she stalked, head held high, from the crowded ante-room crowded with leather-clad clones.

'I hope you're satisfied now!' she gritted to Quinn.

'Don't fret, Rowena, I'm sure your ice-cold bitch image can survive worse than this.'

'I hate you!' If that were true, how it would simplify matters.

'I can live with that,' he lied, increasing his pace to keep up with her. 'It's being ignored I'm not so comfortable with,' he concluded grimly.

'I've heard of men who turn to stalking when they get given the push, but I never thought you'd be one of them, Quinn. If only I'd known then what I know now...' As if it would have made any difference, a self-derisive voice-over in her head insisted on supplementing.

'I haven't been given the push.'

Rowena came to an abrupt halt in front of her PA's desk. Hands planted on her hips, she swung around, causing her silver-blonde hair to bell around her face before settling down into the loosely tendrilled nape-length style she'd recently adopted.

'Consider yourself pushed, Quinn.'

Quinn smiled. 'Like hell I will!' Ignoring her loudly voiced protests, he placed his hand against her chest and thrust her through the open door of her office. 'Hold all Ms Parrish's calls,' he instructed the startled-looking young woman behind the desk.

'Call Security, Bernice!' Rebecca yelled shrilly just before Quinn kicked the door closed. 'I suppose you think this ridiculous caveman act is impressive!' she jeered, retreating to the other side of her large desk—the symbol of her authority. Unfortunately it didn't afford her that warm, in-charge feeling it normally did.

'If you think spending just one night with me entitles you to behave like this you're sadly mistaken, not to mention living in the wrong century. As for taking off your clothes—I'm not even going to ask!' she choked, her nose wrinkling in disgust at the thought of Quinn parading half naked in front of the other women. 'If I hadn't come in when I did, heaven knows how far you'd have gone!'

'And you don't like that idea?' Quinn didn't sound as though her disgust displeased him.

It made her feel sick to the stomach. 'I hate to spoil your pathetic male fantasies of women fighting over you, but I simply don't like the idea of you wasting my staff's time. We have deadlines to meet, you know. How would you like it if I smuggled myself into your hospital and tried to pass myself off as a nurse?'

'Give me a minute here, I'm just picturing you... Does the uniform have one of those cute frilly caps?' Rowena didn't have time to respond to this outrageous piece of sexism before his languid air of mockery vanished, revealing the sort of penetrative expression that made her nostalgic for his irritating mockery of seconds before. 'What the hell have you been doing to yourself, Rowena?' He sat down on the edge of her desk and stretched his long legs out in front of him.

'I had my hair cut.'

'That's not what I mean. You've lost weight.'

'Thank you.'

Her hips had always been the envy of her more amply endowed friends, but losing almost a stone in weight during the past few weeks meant that the short skirt she was wearing today no longer clung to her hips, but hung loosely.

'You look terrible.'

In case I hadn't got the point, she thought caustically.

'You don't lose that sort of weight so quickly unless you're ill or under a lot of pressure,' he announced authoritatively.

Her glance slid evasively from his. Did morning sickness count as being ill? 'Well, thanks for the medical assessment, Doctor, but I'm neither. It's just too many late nights, and no time to eat.'

'In fact life's just one long party.' He didn't bother hiding his scepticism.

'Absolutely,' she maintained defiantly.

'Which no doubt accounts for you ignoring my e-mails and phone calls—although that isn't a problem now, is it? Not since you had all your numbers changed and went ex-directory.' Rowena watched with an irritated frown as he began to mess up the row of pencils laid out symmetrically on her desk. Looking at his long, clever fingers brought a sudden rush of memories, his fingers dark against her pale breasts. His fingers sliding between…

Rowena caught her full lower lip between her teeth. She resented the fact he was making her behave guiltily. 'That was pure coincidence,' she announced with stilted defiance.

He lifted his head, and from beneath the sweep of inky dark lashes looked enquiringly across at her. 'And is it coincidence that had me made *persona non grata* at your apartment building?'

Rowena had a firm policy of ignoring things she couldn't deny and she did so now with a careless toss of her fair head. 'I've only just got back, Quinn. New York was hectic.' She wished straight off she hadn't mentioned New York.

She thought of New York and, unlike normal people who had spent any time there, she didn't associate with the vibrant, alive, noisy, scary, exciting place it was. No, Rowena immediately associated it with Quinn, incredible sex and the frightening consequences of the latter…

'What about the weekend you came home?'

'You knew about that?' Startled, she glanced up to see an expression she couldn't quite place on his face.

'Wasn't I meant to?'

'It was no secret.' Recovering a little composure, Rowena managed to continue in a persuasively reasonable tone. 'I've just started a new job. I've hardly had time to make contact with every casual acquaintance I have.' She gulped, but the sound was drowned out by the sibilant hiss of his indrawn breath.

Oh, God, that had come out all wrong and then some…!

'Casual acquaintance,' he said very softly and deadly silkily. Then, even softer, '*Casual acquaintance.* Tell me, Rowena, how do you say hello to people you know quite well?'

She closed her eyes as an image appeared in her mind's eye of herself walking down the crowded New York street three months ago, surrounded by a seething mass of humanity. Maybe it had been the mild culture shock of moving to another city where she knew nobody, or maybe it had been the stress of proving herself, but she had never felt so alone in her life.

Then she'd seen him. She hadn't even needed to get a proper look at that unmistakable profile—his innately elegant, long-legged stride would have been sufficient proof. Two men in the world couldn't move that way. Without thinking she had barged through the people separating them, breaking every rule of pedestrian etiquette and probably bruising a few shins to get to him.

Waving her bag above her head, she'd shrieked his name like a demented banshee until she'd been hoarse. She'd almost been at his shoulder when he'd finally turned around and

Rowena, her face flushed, breathing hard, had come to an abrupt halt.

Shock of recognition in his eyes had morphed into hot desire. An answering desire had shimmered hot and liquid through her.

'You're here,' she said stupidly. 'I can't believe it.'

And then he kissed her.

'Convinced now?' he asked, when he lifted his head.

Rowena stared dizzily up into his face unable to focus properly—unable to do anything much except stare at him.

The native New Yorkers, a tolerant bunch and not easily surprised, had parted around the embracing couple.

'I always knew you'd be a good kisser, you've got such a beautiful mouth.' Her hands, pressed flat against the hard surface of his chest, felt his responsive rumble of laughter.

He continued to display his proficiency at kissing in the taxi, then in the lift going up to his hotel room. The kissing didn't stop once the door had closed behind them but other things started, things she couldn't even think about without blushing.

Hurtling back into the present, Rowena was still faced with Quinn's anger at being called a casual acquaintance. 'You caught me at a weak moment,' she defended herself.

'There was no catching involved—the way I recall it you did the running.' He reached across and touched her chin with his forefinger.

'And you wonder why I've been avoiding you,' she said, jerking her chin away from his grip.

'I thought that was all in my mind.' Quinn spun around on the smooth surface of the desk until his legs were the wrong side of it—her side.

'I knew it would be like this,' she muttered, grabbing two handfuls of silvery fair hair and shaking her head from side to side. 'I thought you understood New York was a mistake, not the start of something.' Nothing that she had any intention of telling him about just now, anyhow.

'The only mistake I made was allowing you to persuade me to leave.'

Rowena's heart dropped as far as her narrow, expensively shod feet. His inflexible tone and grim expression suggested that he was about to compensate for that mistake.

She closed her eyes, incredibly frustrated by his unyielding, downright mule-headed attitude. 'Talking to you is like...like talking to that wall!'

Which, if things went on like this, she'd be doing in next to no time. She could see it now—crazy fashion editor carted away by the men in white coats. How her enemies would love that...another fast-track hot shot hits the dust!

'You *want* me,' he insisted.

At least this was one subject he didn't have any doubts about—he couldn't be in the same room as her without knowing that Rowena craved his touch just as much as he did hers. This knowledge only increased his frustration. Hell, the sizzling, sexually fuelled static between them was nothing short of a fire hazard!

Rowena glared at him for about twenty seconds before her defiance deserted her. 'That's as maybe,' she conceded, concentrating hard on controlling her wildly fluctuating complexion—women in her position did not blush like schoolgirls; neither did they ache inside the way she did.

Quinn's grin had a worryingly predatory look to it.

'No maybe about it.'

A small shrug of her slender shoulders conceded his cocky claim. 'You've only yourself to blame—laying down rules and conditions,' she brooded darkly. 'Whatever happened to spontaneity and free love?' She quivered, working herself into a resentful lather as she contemplated her bad luck. She'd found the lover of her dreams—a man not noted for his steadfast devotion—and he had to get all moralistic and possessive on her.

'Free love?' Quinn mused. 'I'm trying to see you as a flower child, but it's not easy,' he admitted.

'You're nothing but a reformed rake!' The old-fashioned term seemed to suit him oddly well—he definitely had the legs for tight-fitting Regency breeches as well.

Quinn's lips quivered at this hot accusation. 'Just for the record, in my book spontaneity is good, but you get nothing for free. You'll have to learn to live with the fact I'm not available on a casual, nocturnal basis only. There are people who provide such services, I believe—for a price!'

Her hand flashed out but Quinn's reflexes were faster. Rowena found her wrist enclosed in a steely grip. Feet braced on the floor, he drew her in between the confines of his iron-hard muscular thighs as he pulled her hand back down to her side, clicking his tongue in mocking disapproval.

'I want to be part of your life, Rowena—an integral part.' Rowena stopped struggling, at least physically. Her inner conflict was less easily subdued! Their eyes meshed and she instantly got herself lost in his sea green gaze. 'I've no interest in the sort of hole-in-the-corner affair you were suggesting in New York.'

'Private is not the same as sordid.' Most men would have been flattered by the sort of civilised arrangement she had offered him—no complications, no emotional dramas.

'I'm not good at subterfuge.'

Rowena's bosom swelled with incredulous indignation. 'There speaks the man who'd just conned his way into this building!'

'If you hadn't been so unreasonable I wouldn't have needed to resort to less than open tactics.'

'Dirty tactics, you mean,' she retorted, pulling her wrist free from his grip and waving an admonitory finger in front of his nose. 'We both know that when you want something there's just about nothing you won't do!' she snapped furiously.

Quinn gazed levelly back at her, not the least disturbed by her heated indictment. He reached forward and ran a finger slowly down the soft curve of her cheek, his piercing eyes darkening as she flinched back as if burnt.

'And at the moment I want you…'

Her angry flush faded with dramatic abruptness leaving Rowena marble pale. Her breath emerged as a shaky tremulous gasp. Where was the scornful put-down when she needed one?

'Is that meant to be some sort of turn-on? Well, I've got news for you…' It worked extremely well. 'Your problem is you like everyone to know about your trophy girlfriends,' she jeered hoarsely. 'It makes you feel the big man to see yourself plastered all over the gossip columns.'

'I think that's slight exaggeration, Rowena, I barely rate a couple of lines in *Country Life*.'

'Your false modesty makes me sick.'

'You'll get used to the idea, you know,' he promised.

'What idea?'

'The idea of being part of a couple.'

'And if I don't?'

'You don't have any choice, angel.'

'How do you figure that one?'

'You need me.'

Rowena gasped. His arrogance was simply unbelievable! 'Have you always been delusional?'

His expression abruptly softened as he assimilated the torment in her wide-spaced eyes. 'You need me, about as much as I need you. See, I can do it, and I've had as little practice at it as you have. It hardly hurts at all to admit it. I'm going to teach you to say it,' he promised.

Eyes wide with horror and lips clamped defiantly shut, she shook her head vigorously from side to side.

'We'll see, shall we?'

There was no challenge in his statement, just total, complete conviction—whether this conviction stemmed from a misplaced notion that she was female and therefore weak and malleable, or a belief in his own ability to bend anything or anyone to his will, Rowena didn't know. She did know a challenge would have been much easier to deal with.

Rowena wanted to put him right, but she felt strangely disinclined to do anything, move, speak, breathe even—perhaps it had something to do with the almost narcotic quality of the combination of his level, deep voice and the sexily slumbrous gleam in his eyes.

'I did knock, Rowena…' Her PA's tentative voice made Rowena start.

'Yes, Bernice?' she responded, putting as much clear space rapidly between herself and Quinn as was possible. Her mind wasn't functioning with its usual clarity, but at least she wasn't staring up at him like a hypnotised rabbit screaming 'eat me' any longer.

This was one of the reasons she hadn't wanted to see him. He walked in a room and her wits flew out the nearest window, which made no sense! Rowena had experienced sexual attraction before and stayed firmly in charge of her feelings at every level—the person involved only knew about it if she wanted him to. With Quinn she didn't have that luxury, she was clumsy, inarticulate and painfully *needy*.

'There's a call from your sister and she says it's urgent…'

Rowena frowned. Holly had taken her new fiancé up to Scotland to show him off to their elderly grandparents who lived in a remote part of the country called Wester Ross.

'Fine, I'll take it, Bernice,' Rowena replied to her normally discreet assistant who was shooting surreptitious looks in Quinn's direction.

The young woman withdrew, blushing, when Quinn smiled at her.

'Holly, it's me…do you mind? This is private!' she hissed, covering the mouthpiece and glaring across at Quinn.

'Say hello to Holly for me,' he requested, unperturbed by her hostility as he strolled to the far end of the room and began to read the titles on the spines of the files that filled the shelves there.

'What? Yes, it is Quinn. No…yes, he is here. It doesn't matter, I'll explain later. What's wro—?' Rowena grew silent as her sister broke into impetuous speech the other end of the line.

Rowena had her back turned to him, but Quinn could almost feel her distress as the slim, supple line of her back grew tense. Her next faltering exclamation confirmed his suspicions—Holly didn't have good news.

'Oh, God, no!' Rowena raised her hand to her mouth, compressing the quivering line of her lips—not Gran!

The image of Elspeth Frazer floated before her eyes. Five feet nothing with rosy cheeks, startling blue eyes and snow-white hair, she could have come straight from the glossy illustrations in a book of fairy tales. The illusion of a cosy grandmother was shattered the instant Elspeth opened her mouth. The octogenarian had never suffered fools gladly and, not only did she have a bawdy sense of humour, she possessed a will of iron.

Elspeth had been a consultant paediatrician in the early fifties, when women consultants had been very few and far between. Rowena had left Holly to follow in Gran's footsteps and become a doctor, but nonetheless Elspeth Frazer had been her own inspiration, the person she thought of when the going got tough. Rowena could never understand how a woman like her grandmother, who had fought so hard to get where she wanted, had turned her back on everything and buried herself in general practice in the back of beyond. She'd eventually asked.

'Why, I saw your grandfather, my dear, and I loved him.'

Perplexed, a much younger Rowena had asked, 'Well couldn't he have come to live in the City?'

'He could, but he'd have been unhappy.'

'Well, I'd never do that for a man!'

'We'll see…'

Rowena heard the familiar soft accent in her head and her eyes filled with tears. She blinked back the moisture and forced herself to ask the thing she didn't want to.

'Is she…? Do they think…? Don't cry, Holly, and don't get too technical,' she pleaded as her doctor sister began to go into details about the suspected stroke that their grandmother had suffered that morning.

She wasn't aware that Quinn was beside her until she felt the warm imprint of his hand on her shoulder. No matter what the state of their personal relationship, she wasn't about to reject his support. Rowena was proud, but not stupid—Quinn was the sort of man whom people automatically turned to in a crisis.

She made no objection as he slid a chair under her shaky legs and urged her gently down into it.

She held the receiver a little way from her ear. 'She's crying again.' She gulped, raising tear-filled eyes to his face. 'Holly never cries,' she added, her own lower lip quivering madly.

'Let me have it.'

Rowena relinquished the phone without a second thought. For once she didn't resent Quinn's air of calm authority.

'Hello, Holly, sweetheart, it's Quinn,' she heard him say warmly to her sister. 'Yes, I know, but…is Niall there? Good, put him on. Hi, Niall, it's Quinn.'

Rowena, her head in her hands, could hear the male rumble as Holly's fiancé responded at length. Quinn didn't interrupt him. 'Yes, I get the picture. It'll be quicker if we fly up. Can you organise some transport from Inverness? Right, I'll ring when I've got more details.'

CHAPTER THREE

ROWENA woke up, and for several horrid moments experienced total amnesia. It didn't last long, but realising where she was, with whom and, worst of all, why was no less horrid than the original empty void.

She stretched sleepily in the confined space. There was a dull ache behind her eyes and her stiff limbs felt as though she hadn't moved in an age. A glance at her watch revealed this wasn't far off the truth; they couldn't be far off Inverness.

'You're awake.'

The soft drawl somewhere east of her right ear was extremely welcome, not that she had any intention of allowing her travelling companion to see just how welcome. 'Very obviously.' Rowena raised a hand to cover her yawn as she adjusted her seat from its reclining position. Someone, she noticed, had placed a blanket over her while she'd slept. Had it been Quinn? The thought made her throat feel achey and tight. God, this has to stop, she rebuked herself sharply. Carry on broadcasting emotional and vulnerable signals like these and they'll pick them up in the Shetlands, girl!

'How are you feeling?' With raised brows Quinn took in her aggressive frown. 'Other than grouchy.'

'I'm not grouchy.'

Was she particularly shallow? Or was it normal to fret stupidly about trivial matters like the fact your hair was sticking up and your eyeshadow had probably run when you were on a mission that should, and did, take precedence over everything else? How was there room in her head, given her anxiety levels over Gran, to take on board the fact that Quinn looked overpoweringly virile and as vital and energetic as she felt jaded and weary?

'And I feel perfectly fine.' It occurred to her that she ought to be displaying more gratitude than she was, considering what he had done for her. 'Thank you,' she added awkwardly.

There was no polite way of putting it—she had fallen apart! It was still kind of shocking to accept that this had happened—maybe if Quinn hadn't been there she would have pulled herself together and done what needed to be done.... Perhaps it was the security of having someone she trusted to take care of her and the situation that had enabled her to temporarily relinquish her iron control.

Her blue eyes fluttered wide with amazement; she did trust Quinn—utterly! When, she wondered, had that happened? Aware of his questioning regard, she lowered her eyes abruptly and began to fold the discarded blanket, her slim fingers trembling slightly as she fussed, lining the corners up with meticulous precision.

It was herself she didn't trust! If she allowed sexual attraction to dictate her actions, Rowena knew she wouldn't be doing either of them any favours. Quinn deserved a woman who could give him the things he probably didn't even know he wanted yet. Things like a home—not just four walls and a roof, but a *real* home. There would be babies, of course—*babies*!

Talk about catch-22, she thought, resisting the impulse to place her hands protectively over her belly. Is this really *me* feeling wistful over a dewy-eyed version of domestic bliss…? She shook her head—this had to stop before she started listening to that voice in her head that kept saying a child needed two parents.

You couldn't make a decision on the basis of physical attraction. If she did that she might even, in a moment of weakness and self-delusion, convince herself she could provide what Quinn wanted. The result would be disaster—she'd end up resenting him from stopping her doing what she wanted to do in her career, and in turn he'd resent her because she wouldn't be able to put him first. Quinn was a man who needed to be put first.

'I didn't mean to fall asleep.'

His eyes skimmed her delicately flushed face. 'No problem,' he responded easily.

'I'm not used to drinking brandy in the middle of the day.' Actually she wasn't used to drinking it at any time, which was why the tiny amount she'd had had gone straight to her head. The stuff Quinn had discovered in her kitchen cupboard had been for culinary purposes only up to that afternoon.

'I'd say you're not used to drinking much any time,' Quinn mused with his usual perception. 'But you make a fairly amiable drunk.'

Maybe she was being paranoid, but it seemed to Rowena that his expression hinted at some private joke. She just hoped she hadn't said or done anything too awful or disastrously revealing when she was being *amiable*.

'I'm sorry about the fuss with Security...' Fuss was a pretty mild way of putting it. It was ironic, really—normally she would have applauded their stubborn attempts to detach her from Quinn.

It had actually taken Rowena some time to convince the suspicious employees anxious to do their duty that a kidnap was not in progress. She closed her eyes, mortified to even think about that terrible scene when they'd attempted to leave the magazine offices.

Give it twenty-four hours and the already juicy tale would have been embellished beyond recognition.

'Bernice is a bit overprotective.'

'So I gathered,' Quinn responded drily.

'You did have...' Rowena felt her colour rise but doggedly she continued '...your arm around me.' She saw no reason to remind him or herself how hard she had been clinging to it!

'Kidnapping seems a pretty drastic leap to make.'

'Well, she did see us arguing,' she reminded him in Bernice's defence. 'And I'm not normally the sort of person who goes around leaning on...*anyone*.'

'I'm touched you made an exception in my case.'

Rowena hardly noticed his wry interjection. 'I can't believe I just walked out like that.'

'You were in shock.'

Rowena's expression made it clear that shock was a poor excuse in her eyes for deserting her post.

'What will people think?'

'Do you care?'

'Of course I care, this is my professional reputation we're talking about.' Somehow she doubted if Quinn would be quite so laid back if it were his job they were discussing. 'And in my business,' she told him grimly, 'there's always someone willing to stab you in the back.'

'Perhaps we should ask them to turn the plane around.'

'Don't patronise me, Quinn!' she flared. 'I want to go to see Gran, of course I do. I just wish I'd been thinking straight. I should at least have had the common courtesy to explain to Bernice, she would have cancelled my appointments…' She frowned, trying to recall her busy schedule for the next few days.

'Well, it's not too late, is it?' he pointed out practically. 'And if you're fretting about working I did pack your laptop.'

Rowena could have done without this reminder that, not only had Quinn arranged a private flight, treating the whole procedure as though it were no different from hiring a car, when he'd discovered that there were no seats available on the scheduled departures, but he had also packed her clothes too.

Anaesthetised by the small glass of brandy he had forced between her bloodless lips, she had watched him from her cross-legged position on her bed, occasionally shouting instructions in what she seemed to recall had been a loud and stroppy tone.

'Not those pants, decorative but *far* too uncomfortable!' she'd explained as he'd pulled out a racy-looking thong from her knicker drawer to add to the clothes crammed in her case.

The memory made her groan and clutch her head.

'Could you do with a coffee?' her attentive escort asked.

Escort...*hell*! Quinn on escort duty meant hours and hours of contact, and far too much opportunity for her to let things slip... It was nothing short of miraculous that she hadn't so far!

The last shreds of muddled sleepiness left her as, galvanised into action, she shot upright, and, discovering there was nowhere much to go, sat down again with a bump.

'You can't come to Scotland!' she exclaimed in an anguished tone. She really must have been out of it earlier to have let him get on the plane with her!

'Short of parachuting I've not much option at this point.'

'Obviously you'll be flying straight back.'

Quinn looked down into her worried face and smiled—but it wasn't a comforting sort of smile.

'I promised Niall—'

Rowena's expression hardened. What was this, some male conspiracy. 'Niall had no right to ask you anything. I don't need a minder!'

A lick of flame appeared in his eyes as they stilled on her angry face. 'No, you need a lover of the live-in variety!' Then he smiled benignly and patted her on the back as she began to choke. 'I promised Niall that I'd see you safely to the hospital,' he intoned virtuously.

'Like you never break a promise,' Rowena snarled, placing the glass of water she'd taken several panicky gulps from down again.

His steady green gaze captured and held her furtive, darting glance. 'Actually, no, I don't.'

A slow, steady pulse of heat throbbed through Rowena, infiltrating every individual cell. She could hear the rasp of his voice in her head. '*You'll like this*, I promise.' He'd said it more than once before he'd introduced her to a new sensual experience that had reduced her to incoherent, babbling worship. He'd not broken his promise or exaggerated a claim once that night.

'Some escort you'd be,' she croaked, trying to fight her way through the sexual thrall. She was pretty sure that it had her staring at him like some sex-starved bimbo. 'You don't even know where Gran and Grandpa live.'

'Actually I do, but I'm having a job getting my tongue around the Gaelic pronunciation. A musical language, but not exactly phonetic.'

The way she recalled it, his tongue could be pretty amazingly dextrous! Rowena, her expression fixed and horrified, barely stifled a groan at this fresh evidence of her moral disintegration.

'And it wouldn't really matter if my geographical knowledge of the Highlands was nil, would it? Because we're not heading for your grandparents' home.'

Rowena thought it wise to establish pretty quickly, for her own benefit as much as Quinn's, that there was no *we*.

'Precisely. Even *I* am capable of getting from the airport to the hospital.'

'You might well be right, but unfortunately it's not going to be that easy…'

Rowena's expression grew warily suspicious.

'The plane's been diverted to Glasgow. Inverness is closed due to bad weather.'

'Weather!' She squinted through the window into the darkness. 'What weather?'

'It's snowing.'

'They can't close a whole airport just because of a bit of snow.' Rowena's scornful smile wobbled as panic flared hotly through her.

Not only did this mean it would take even longer to reach Gran, but she would be lumbered with Quinn all the way. Being in the confines of a plane cabin with him was bad enough, but a car was *way* too intimate!

'I suspect it might be more than a *bit*, Rowena.'

She rubbed her clenched knuckles across her chin and let her head fall back. 'This is all I need!' she groaned.

The lush sweep of Quinn's long eyelashes concealed his expression as his eyes moved over the exposed pale length of her slender throat.

'I'll get you there, Rowena.' Quinn, who had always considered himself a reasonably law-abiding, honest type of man was vaguely shocked to recognise just how far he'd be prepared to go to fulfil this promise. For Rowena he wouldn't just bend the rules—he'd break them without a second thought.

Rowena's head snapped up. 'Why bother? This is all working out just how you wanted, isn't it?' she flung recklessly at him.

Annoyance scored Quinn's high cheekbones with dark colour as his deep-set eyes found hers.

'Right now you need to reach your seriously ill grandmother. Do you honestly think I'd welcome seeing that moment delayed when I know how important it is to you?' His lips thinned in fastidious disgust. 'What sort of opportunist loser do you take me for, Rowena…?'

Rowena squirmed beneath his penetrating icy glare. 'Hell,' she reflected with a shudder, 'I wouldn't like to be a medical student you take a dislike to…not that you would take a dislike to anyone, because I'm *sure* you're totally objective and impartial and you wouldn't even *dream* of abusing your power in such a petty way.' Studying his face, she couldn't decide if the faint quiver she saw around his lips was wishful thinking. 'In case you're wondering, this is my way of saying sorry…'

When he stared back at her, stony-faced, Rowena gave a grunt of exasperation. 'For heaven's sake, I think you can afford to be big about this! Cut me a bit of slack, Quinn. I don't know what I'm saying right now, I'm so emotionally whacked!' she admitted wearily.

It would have taken a man with a lot more objectivity than Quinn to remain unmoved by the appeal in those deep blue eyes. 'Consider the slack cut.'

Rowena heaved a relieved sigh, grateful to see Quinn had finally come down off his high horse. 'Can't you do *something*?' she asked wistfully.

'Your faith in my ability is moving, but I have to admit I think you're overestimating my influence in the weather department.' He regretted his levity as Rowena, her lips trembling, buried her face in her hands.

'This is terrible,' she sobbed. 'What if I'm too late? What if she is…?' She stopped, unable to say it, unable to think it!

'Don't worry,' he soothed, stroking her glossy hair. 'I'll get you up to Inverness somehow.'

His offer had the opposite effect to that he'd been striving for. Rowena, her body rigid, shot bolt upright. Her brimming eyes were awash with agitated anguish.

'You *can't*...you...you can't come.'

'Why?'

'You don't even have any suitable clothes,' she added in the manner of someone desperate to produce a winning argument—the desperation wasn't feigned.

Her glance automatically dropped. Quinn had removed his jacket during the flight, and she could see the muscle definition of his chest and even get a hint of the dark body hair through the thin cotton of his white T-shirt. The prickle just beneath her skin reached the surface, she felt the heat bloom in her cheeks and squirmed restlessly in her seat.

When she managed to wrench her gaze back up—there was some time lapse here—Quinn was watching her with a pleased, *knowing* expression on his dark, sexy features that only served to increase the hot flow of blood to her cheeks.

'I picked up some things at the airport.'

'You can't have, you didn't leave me.'

'I didn't need to—I used the services of a very nice airport employee whose sole aim in life is to spend people's money. I gave the person my size and my requirements and they did the rest.'

Rowena knew instinctively that this person had been female and attractive. 'I suppose she took your inside leg measurements too,' she heard herself bitch waspishly. No wonder he looked complacent. Could I sound any more jealous if I tried? she anguished. 'Silk shirts, ties and socks won't be much good. This isn't some soft, safe southern village we're heading for, this is the north of Scotland in the winter,' she told him scornfully. 'And I can get to Inverness myself, thank you very much.'

'You think you're more suited to driving in the north of Scotland than I am? As a matter of interest, when was the last time you drove a car, Rowena?'

'I find public transport convenient. *I do!*' she added defiantly as he gave a sceptical snort.

Not getting your licence until the fourth attempt was not *that* unusual. What was unusual was Rowena not succeeding at something she set her mind to with her usual effortless ease.

'Besides, there's enough pollution,' she added loftily. 'I'm doing my bit for the environment.'

'Very public spirited of you.'

'All right,' she conceded crossly. 'I may not *like* driving, but I'm a very good driver. I'm just *careful*, is all…'

'I'm not contesting it,' he soothed silkily. 'It's purely a personal foible of mine, but I get jumpy when the driver of a car I'm a passenger in closes her eyes when manoeuvring past a large lorry.'

'It was a very narrow bridge.' And a very big lorry.

'I've seen you drive around a car park for half an hour rather than reverse into a parking space.'

'Are you eventually going to make a point?'

One dark brow lifted sardonically. 'I thought I already had.'

Rowena gritted her teeth; she hated his maddening calm. 'It's preposterous. I mean, *obviously* you can't walk out on your life just because…'

'You need me?' He slid a hand behind his head, mussing up his rich dark hair as he settled comfortably back in his seat. 'Actually, nothing could be easier,' he announced carelessly.

There was nothing careless or soothing about the burning expression in the green eyes that welded with hers. Rowena clutched nervously at her tight throat as her thundering heart tried to fight its way out of her chest. She cleared her throat; anyone would think she was the sort of woman that got all turned on by all that predatory, possessive macho nonsense!

'Well, I don't want you,' she announced tautly. The last thing she needed was to be even further in his debt. No, relying on Quinn would be a fatal mistake.

Quinn appeared to take her rejection in his stride. 'Your problem is you don't know what's good for you.'

Was he suggesting that he'd be good for her…? This wasn't a proposition Rowena felt up to challenging.

'Gran always said that to me too. Like you, she's big on clichés, but only when she says them…' For a moment fear, dark and cold, blanked out every other consideration. 'Do you think…?' she whispered, her eyes darkening with dread.

Quinn, his expression compassionate, took hold of her hands now tortuously twisted in her lap and chafed the chilly extremities between his. 'Cold hands, warm heart?' he suggested.

'The exception that proves the rule, that's me,' Rowena responded, unable to stop her teeth from chattering.

'You asked me what I think. For what it's worth, I think it's useless to speculate on your grandmother's condition at this point. She's in the best possible place and she's being cared for by the best possible people.'

Rowena nodded; what he said made perfect sense. 'You're right,' she conceded. 'It's just hard…' she broke off as the emotional lump in her throat became unmanageable.

'You're really fond of your grandparents, aren't you?'

The note of surprise in his voice brought an angry sparkle to Rowena's eyes. Aren't pushy, upwardly mobile bitches allowed to care for their families? she wanted to yell. She snatched her hands from his and pushed her hair back behind her ears. 'Why should that surprise you?'

'It doesn't surprise me, Rowena, though I can think of several people it might surprise. You play your glacial ice-maiden part extremely well.'

Rowena opened her mouth to contest this description then, realising he had a point, shrugged in tired resignation.

'Tell me about them,' he urged unexpectedly.

'Gran and Grandpa?' Her neatly shaped brows drew together in straight line. *'Why?'*

'Do you always suspect people's motives?' he responded, a hint of exasperation in his tone. 'I've no sinister hidden agenda, Rowena. You need to talk, and I…I want to listen.'

'Grandpa owned a trawler before he retired.'

'Fishing is a high-risk profession.'

'And not a very lucrative one these days. Grandpa's old boat has been tarted up to take tourists on trips around the Summer Isles these days. Grandpa doesn't say so but I think he finds that quite sad. Mind you, he doesn't say much full stop, but he's always been there for me,' she added swiftly, just in case Quinn was mistakenly associating strong and silent with strong and unfeeling. 'He's unfailingly supportive…never judgemental. A quiet *gentle* giant.' Her eyes misted with affection.

'And your grandmother…?' Quinn prompted gently.

'Oh, she's not quiet, in fact she's the total opposite to Grandpa, but somehow they are *right* together, if you know what I mean…?' She was so involved in her own private reflections that she didn't see Quinn nod. 'I just can't imagine them apart. Gran always encouraged Holly and I to…' She wiped the tears from her cheeks with the back of her hand. 'Sorry.'

Quinn pressed a tissue into her hand. 'They sound great; I'd love to meet them.'

'Oh, they'd like you,' she said, enthusiastically, without thinking. Her jaw dropped in almost comical dismay as their eyes met. 'That is…' she laughed awkwardly as she lowered her gaze hastily from his '…what's not to like? You're an adorable sort of guy,' she joked shakily.

'That's what I've been trying to tell you.'

If she wasn't careful he might realise how successful he'd been! 'I don't usually cry so much…'

'Your "don't get mad, get even" policy doesn't really cover this situation, does it, angel?'

Choked up, Rowena shook her head. 'Not really. Oh, God!' She groaned. 'I should be there. When I think of Gran all alone…'

'She's hardly alone, is she?'

'No, that's true. Mum and Dad are there, that's a good thing. Isn't it?'

'Of course it is, and Holly and Niall are there too—quite the family gathering.'

Rowena sensed his unspoken question. 'I was invited. It's Grandpa's birthday tomorrow and Holly wanted to show Niall off. I couldn't justify taking a break…'

If Quinn detected the guilt in her voice he didn't comment on it.

'I was surprised to find out about Holly and Niall…' Quinn's light comment invited a response, which Rowena didn't give. If he had been surprised, she'd been shocked rigid by the news that Holly was to marry someone she had always considered one of her own best friends.

It wasn't as if she grudged her baby sister her happiness, or that she felt she had any particular claims on Niall who, like Quinn, had been her friend since university days—she had been there for him after his first marriage had broken up. It just took some major readjusting, that was all.

Quinn's watchful eyes remained on her downcast features. 'It was all a bit quick, wasn't it?' He thought he managed to hide his suspicions pretty well under the circumstances—the circumstances being he was highly suspicious of Rowena's relationship with Niall.

'They seem very happy,' Rowena eventually responded carefully.

The lines bracketing Quinn's strong mouth deepened as his lips tightened. 'And if you had any doubts, you wouldn't say so. Being that sour grapes sound so…well, *sour*.'

Rowena was bewildered by the abrupt change of mood she sensed in him. 'Meaning what, exactly?' she gritted dangerously.

'I always had the impression that you considered you had first refusal on Niall,' he drawled.

Rowena took a deep, wrathful breath. The problem was, there was a grain of truth in his abominable charge—not that she had ever had a romantic relationship with Niall, nor for that matter had she ever wanted one, but they had been close. Closer probably in their post-student days than she and Quinn had been.

Possibly, Rowena mused, considering the matter in a new light, because there never had been any of the unacknowledged physical attraction between her and Niall that there was between her and Quinn. It was nice to go places with a very attractive man and not have to worry that he'd expect anything at the end of the evening other than stimulating conversation and good coffee.

'Niall is everything you are not,' she announced scornfully.

Though experienced in relationships with the opposite sex, Quinn was not experienced in jealousy. It was like an open wound, which he couldn't help poking even though it hurt. 'And what am I, Rowena? Other than not being fit to lick Niall's boots, that is. Is it Niall's title you begrudge Holly?'

'Are you *trying* to insult me?'

'Did you fancy yourself as part of the landed gentry? Well, marrying Niall would certainly give you that,' he admitted, reviewing their mutual friend's blue-blooded background.

'I never wanted to marry Niall.'

'Did he ask?'

Rowena flushed angrily.

'I see he didn't.'

'He didn't ask me to marry him, the same way he never took advantage of our friendship and made a pass at me! Unlike *some* people I could mention!'

'Am I being unduly sensitive or was that little jibe aimed at me? If so, I feel obliged to say in my defence that the way I recall it, sweetheart, you were pretty anxious to be taken advantage of,' he reminded her with unforgivable accuracy.

'Just for the record, I do not begrudge Holly anything!' Rowena snapped, finding it hard not to lose her rag totally in the face of extreme provocation.

'Sure you don't.'

'I don't!' she bellowed back, unable to take his tolerant contempt any longer. 'And as for what you are, that's simple, Quinn. You are the most arrogant, infuriating, *manipulative* male I've ever met—and in case you have any doubts, that wasn't a compliment!' she finished, lifting a hand to her hot, sticky brow. 'I'm stuck with you as far as Glasgow,' she stormed, 'but after that I'm going on alone.'

Quinn, unfazed by her animosity, just smiled in that laconic, laid-back, wildly attractive way of his and announced his intention of snatching a few minutes' sleep. He seemed to drift into a deep, untroubled slumber about two seconds after his eyes closed and, much to her chagrin, stayed that way until the attractive flight attendant woke him to fasten his seat belt.

Their plane was about the last one to land—quite bumpily, as it happened, as the nail marks gouged in Quinn's hand from where Rowena had gripped it could testify—before the airport ground to a total standstill. The blizzards that had cut off the far north had, it seemed, reached Glasgow.

'I don't know why you're following me,' Rowena remarked icily to the tall figure at her shoulder.

'I'm only here as an interested bystander, but should you require my services…'

'I won't.'

'Sorry to keep you waiting, miss,' the harassed-looking individual behind the car-hire counter apologised. 'We don't have a four-wheel drive left…'

Rowena tapped her beautifully manicured nails on the desk. 'Then what do you have?' she enquired with barely disguised impatience.

The young man told her.

'That'll do.'

'It's snowing…'

'I had noticed.' The recipient of her abrasive sarcasm flushed and, feeling guilty, Rowena smiled tightly to take the sting out of her words.

The smile only further flustered the young man who shot the intimidatingly beautiful blonde's companion a look of appeal, but the tall man shrugged and remained silent.

'Well, actually, the police are advising people who don't have to make a journey to stay at home…most people are…'

'I'm not most people, and I do have to make a journey,' Rowena responded, disguising her increasing sense of urgency behind a cold façade.

'Well, perhaps you could wait until morning?' One look from those icy eyes silenced the young man. Clearly unhappy, he dropped the keys into her outstretched palm. 'How far are you planning to go?'

'Inverness.'

His eyes widened. 'You're joking—right!'

'If you knew the lady better, you wouldn't bother asking that.'

Rowena spun around. This wasn't the first time today Quinn had insinuated she had no sense of humour. She had a *great* sense of humour!

'Nobody asked you, Quinn Tyler!'

Quinn regarded her angry face impassively. 'I can take a hint.'

Rowena laughed bitterly. 'Since when?'

'Just remember, keep in the highest gear possible when driving on snow and don't brake in a skid, steer into it,' he advised her gravely.

'I knew that!' she called after him.

Rowena watched the tall retreating figure and experienced none of the deep sense of relief she should have; she only felt a nasty sinking feeling in the pit of her stomach. Her chin up, she took a deep sustaining breath. She was alone and she would cope, she told herself sternly, just as she always had.

This sense of stubborn optimism lasted until she passed the seventh abandoned vehicle slewed horribly across the road. It was while her attention was distracted by the desolate image that her own car hit a patch of black ice and began to move in the wrong direction. Panic took over—she had no control whatsoever.

Quinn held his breath as the silver Saab ahead went into a dramatic skid—the whole scene was picked up in stomach-churning detail by the light of the taxi's headlights. He began to breathe again as it came to an abrupt halt on what had once been a grassy verge.

'How much do I owe you?' he asked the taxi driver who had been following Rowena's car at a discreet distance.

The driver named a hair-raising sum. Quinn, who had agreed to paying quadruple the going rate to persuade the reluctant driver to venture out, didn't blink as he handed over the exorbitant sum.

'I told you not to brake,' he shouted above the howl of the wind as he ducked his head inside the car.

Rowena's first thought was for the baby. Fortunately the only part of her that had suffered from the abrupt stop was her forehead, which had glanced against the windscreen. With a relieved sigh, she pushed back her hair from her face and lifted her head off the steering wheel as a blast of cold air and a flurry of snow hit her.

The dazed expression in her eyes wasn't entirely due to impact; the brush with danger had released a flood of protective maternal instincts as powerful as they were unanticipated. *The baby's all right, the baby's all right.* Like a record stuck in the groove, the relieved litany kept going around and around in her head.

Blinking, she stared up in disbelief at the tall dynamic figure who had wrenched open the car door. She shivered; the nervous sweat that bathed her body was swiftly growing clammily cold in the icy temperature.

What she wanted to say was, I'm glad to see you! Our baby's all right. What she actually said, in a crossly accusing tone, was, 'How did you get here?'

Quinn flung his bag in the back seat. 'Never mind that, slide over,' came the terse instruction.

Normally Rowena would have objected in the strongest possible terms to being addressed so peremptorily, only right now she was too stressed out by the nightmare few miles she'd driven to think coherently. Conscious only of a deep sense of relief, she meekly did as Quinn instructed. The noise level of the growling wind was deadened to a dull roar as he closed the door behind him.

'You're bleeding,' he remarked quietly.

'Am I?'

Quinn's dark skin tones looked peculiarly pale in the subdued light inside the car. Still dazed, Rowena winced slightly as his long, square-tipped fingers gently probed the bruised area on her temple.

She remained passive during the examination, but her near-death experience didn't stop her stomach muscles clenching painfully as the enclosed space started to fill up with a warm male, uniquely Quinn fragrance. She lowered her eyes self-consciously and watched the snow melt on the shoulders of his jacket—

Quinn had the sort of shoulders that filled out jackets extremely well.

'It's only superficial,' he announced clinically.

'I think I must have hit my head on the windscreen.'

A muscle in his lean cheek did some unauthorised jumping. 'You could have killed yourself!' No clinical objectivity this time!

Rowena recoiled from the white-hot blaze of outrage in his eyes.

'Well, I didn't,' she pointed out mildly. 'So there's no point stressing out over what might have happened.'

Their eyes meshed and an explosive sound of frustration escaped from between Quinn's clenched teeth.

'You are totally unbelievable. You're not going to admit you were wrong, are you?'

'It's not something I'm good at, but then neither are you,' she felt impelled to add.

Quinn grunted. 'I'm driving you to the nearest hotel.' He lifted his cell phone from his pocket and began to punch in a number. 'I'll let Niall know what's happening. Hell!' He glared at the inanimate object in his hand. 'There's no reception.'

'Just as well, because I'm not stopping at a hotel. I'm going to Inverness.'

Quinn regarded her set stubborn expression with an expression of frustrated incredulity.

'I can't decide if you're just stubborn or plain stupid.'

'There's no need to get offensive.'

He shook his head. 'You're not going to do your grandmother or anyone else any good if you manage to get yourself killed, woman. You do realise that, I suppose?'

Rowena did, but the compulsion to reach her grandmother was so strong that it pushed every other consideration to the back of her mind.

It was partly a guilt thing, of course, some objective corner of her mind admitted freely. Her grandfather's birthday wasn't the first family occasion she'd missed. If it was too late to make up for all the times she *hadn't* made this journey—the times when she'd put her career ahead of family commitment—Rowena knew she'd never be able to live with herself.

Please let me have a second chance, she begged silently. Rowena was all too aware that second chances came along rarely.

'If you're too scared to drive me I'll drop you off at the next service station,' she declared.

Quinn searched her pale face and saw not an inch of give in her zealot-like determination. He shrugged.

'If you've got a death wish, far be it from me to frustrate you.'

CHAPTER FOUR

'THAT'S it, then.' Quinn loosened his seat belt and leant back in his seat with a sigh. He pressed a finger to the permanent indentation between his dark brows; his head ached dully after the lengthy period of intense concentration.

Rowena looked from Quinn's remote profile to the snow silently building up on the windscreen.

'It can't be!' she cried, adjusting the angle of the overhead light as she consulted the map that lay open on her lap. 'There *must* be another way. It stands to reason.' Even as she spoke Rowena recognised the futility of her protest.

Quinn reached across and closed the book. 'This car isn't going any farther, Rowena,' he said gently. 'We're stuck.' So far closed roads and the police had made them re-route three times, and gradually they'd got farther and farther off their original route.

'But...'

Quinn shook his head firmly.

The snow had now completely covered the windscreen, lending an eerie white glow to the interior of the car. Even though the heater was pumping out heat, Rowena shivered.

'It's not negotiable, sweetheart, we're stuck. We'll just have to sit tight until someone rescues us. It'll be light in an hour or so.' They wouldn't be the only ones waiting for rescue; they'd passed several vehicles along the way in a similar predicament.

'And when will that be, do you think?' Rowena quavered hoarsely as her mind began to actively contemplate the hours ahead. It wasn't the physical discomforts of the situation that filled her with horror. Actually, horror was inadequate to describe her feelings as she thought about the hours ahead stranded in the car with Quinn. Her stomach muscles, sensitive to the frisson of sexual heat that shot through her tensed frame, tightened.

Quinn shrugged. 'I've no idea,' he admitted, shifting his position to ease the tension that was tying the muscles in his neck in knots.

His mellow soothing tone irritated the hell out of Rowena. 'Don't you care?'

'Naturally I care, I just don't see much point getting hysterical. Or would you prefer me to panic?' A nerve in his cheek thrummed as he recalled how close he'd been to doing so when her car had gone into that skid.

Quinn panicking—no, I don't think so! Another time the idea would have made her laugh. Quinn was cool and competence personified.

'I'm sure this is nothing to a man who makes life and death decisions for a living, but humour me, Quinn, I'm only the girl who writes about the latest fashion craze!'

One dark brow quirked as he shifted in his seat to face her properly. 'Do I detect a shade of disillusionment…?' he wondered, sounding surprised.

'You do not!' she denied forcefully. She moderated her tone, aware she could be accused of sounding like the lady who protesteth just a tad too much. 'And, just for the record, I am not getting hysterical. I'm merely showing a *normal* degree of concern. What are you doing now?'

'I'm going to make sure the exhaust is clear of snow,' he explained, zipping his jacket up to his chin. 'The last thing we need is the car filling up with carbon monoxide. You stay put,' he added, fishing a torch from his pocket.

Rowena sketched an angry mock salute, which he acknowledged with an undisturbed grin. Where, she felt like asking, did he think she was about to go? She rubbed a small hole in the condensation that had built up on her window, and, nose almost pressed to the glass, watched him make his way to the rear of the vehicle through the thigh-deep snow that surrounded their stranded vehicle.

Waiting impatiently for him to reappear, she exhaled against the glass and began to idly doodle in the fogged window. It wasn't until she saw his tall figure re-materialise that she registered what she'd drawn on the glass. A giant heart pierced with an arrow and the initials RP and QT inside it stared accusingly back at her.

With a horrified gasp Rowena rubbed out the childish, incriminating evidence and settled back in her seat before the door opened—either she was exhibiting early symptoms of cabin fever or her subconscious was in a sorry state!

'Sorted,' Quinn revealed a short time later as, shaking his head to release the snow clinging to his dark hair and eyelashes, he slid smoothly back into his seat. 'Next we let the appropriate authorities know where we are.'

Rowena only had the vaguest of ideas who the appropriate authorities might be, but Quinn seemed confident he did. She watched as he withdrew his phone from his breast pocket and punched in a number.

'The battery's too low,' he revealed after a few fruitless attempts.

Rowena folded her arms protectively across her chest and discovered she was shaking. 'Well, that's just great, isn't it?'

'So this is my fault now, is it?'

Rowena flushed with guilt and caught her lower lip between her teeth as she encountered his ironic, irritated stare. Did he think she needed it spelling out that she was to blame for their predicament?

To her discomfort he pursued the topic further. 'I suppose you'd prefer to be stuck in the middle of nowhere alone…?'

Rowena gulped. 'Is that where we are?' she whispered fearfully. 'In the middle of nowhere?' This wouldn't have come as a shock to a brighter person, she concluded, averting her eyes from the emptiness of the dark bleak landscape outside her window.

'You tell me, you were the navigator.'

She looked so stricken that Quinn wished he'd resisted the temptation to wind her up. Actually it wasn't Rowena he was annoyed with, it was himself. He couldn't blame his own actions on ignorance; it had been obvious from the outset that this insane journey had been doomed to failure. The only thing that had persuaded him to play ball was the sneaking suspicion that Rowena was quite capable of bribing some other idiot to help her if he didn't—or, worse still, trying the journey on her own the minute his back was turned! The problem was Rowena was just too used to getting her own way.

'Well, actually, I sort of lost track…' One dark brow rose satirically as she fumbled for words. 'All right,' she conceded with a sigh. 'I've not the faintest idea where we are.'

'I've got a confession to make too…'

I bet it's not as spectacular as the one I've got to make some time soon! How long, Rowena wondered bleakly, was she going to be able to keep her secret? It didn't help when every time she looked at Quinn her conscience gave her hell. She silently cursed the cruel fate that had conspired to throw them together this way. How could she tell Quinn she was expecting his baby when she still hadn't had time to come to terms with it herself?

'I already kind of suspected that you had no idea where we were.'

'Because I'm a female and therefore incapable of reading a map, I suppose.'

'It was a joke, Rowena. The usual response is a laugh—you ought to try it some time.' His eyes drifted towards her mouth. His body responded helplessly to the sight of the soft pink contours.

'I don't know how you can joke about something like this,' she choked, lifting resentful eyes to his face and discovering in the process that he didn't look amused. His shifting expression revealed a totally unexpected gleam of raw hunger and hurriedly she looked away, her heart thudding scarily fast. 'There is nothing even vaguely amusing about this situation as far as I can see,' she said, forcing the words past the aching congested feeling in her throat.

She viewed a mental graph charting her day's achievements—it didn't make happy reading. She'd set out to escape Quinn and reach Gran—she'd failed spectacularly on both counts.

One minor consolation, she thought, was when you hit rock bottom things couldn't get worse…

Quinn looked slightly taken aback by her hissing animosity. 'Never heard of laughing in the face of adversity, Rowena?'

Rowena snorted and refused point-blank to respond to his cajoling words or meet his eyes.

'Well, I always say—'

'Something deep and profound, no doubt,' she muttered.

One dark brow quirked but he didn't respond to her sarcasm. 'Don't waste time worrying over things you have no control over.'

'Profound…I was right.'

Annoyance stirred deep in Quinn's emerald eyes. 'This situation will be a lot easier to endure if you keep the smart backchat and cynicism to the bare minimum.'

Rowena heard the unspoken *or else* in his voice and her jaw tightened belligerently.

'It would be a lot easier,' she snapped back, 'if you didn't treat me like a child.'

'Have you listened to yourself lately, sweetheart? I've heard more mature comments from sulky seven-year-olds.' Rowena flushed in annoyance as she reluctantly acknowledged there was more than a little justification in his accusation. 'I know you're anxious about your grandmother, but sitting here feeling sorry for ourselves and scoring points isn't going to get us far.'

And pretending nothing was wrong would?

'No, that'll take a snowplough, and I'm *not* feeling sorry for myself.'

Quinn's arm brushed against her leg as he leaned between their seats into the rear of the car, and the brief contact made her hopelessly responsive nerve endings surge into tingling life. Rowena couldn't control the survival instinct that made her shrink protectively back in her seat—she hoped Quinn hadn't noticed.

'What are you doing now?' she asked.

He shot her a brief, unsmiling glance.

'Concentrating on some of those things we *do* have some control over.' He hefted his holdall onto his lap and unzipped it. 'The petrol's low, so we can't leave the engine running indefinitely. It's going to get cold so we should add a few layers.' He pulled out several items of clothing. Snapping a sales tag off a crew-necked lightweight thermal fleece, he dropped it in Rowena's lap.

'Put that one on. It may not be your first choice in this season's leisure wear but it's better than hypothermia. Besides, if we don't stay warm we might be obliged to raise our body temperatures in the good old-fashioned, time-tested manner…'

Rowena rubbed the fine smooth fabric absently between her fingers. Her blue eyes remained innocently uncomprehending; the faintest suggestion of a frown line above her neat aquiline nose deepened fractionally as their glances collided.

'Skin to skin contact,' he elaborated. The mocking smile that revealed a set of even white teeth didn't reach his eyes. 'The last resort…or the first, depending on your point of view…'

A rosy bloom washed away the pearly, almost opalescent sheen of her fair skin.

'Oh!' In her head she could see the contrast of pale fair skin against dark olive-toned flesh… She blinked hard to dispel the disturbing images.

'And I got the impression just now you wouldn't welcome that.' He couldn't keep the bitterness from his voice. It was not encouraging to have the woman he was running after cringe away from his touch.

He had noticed her shrinking back in her seat and now he thought she didn't *like* him touching her! How ironic was that?

'I could tell you how my skin craves your touch...' She cleared her throat and her voice unexpectedly fell from faltering falsetto to husky rasp. 'But I'm afraid, Quinn, I don't have the time or inclination to soothe fragile male egos!' Her scornful glare grew limp around the edges as she saw her contemptuous sarcasm had not cut him to the quick. Actually, all of a sudden he was oozing very male satisfaction and looking scarily confident!

'Don't worry, Rowena, I haven't made out in a car since I was a teenager, and I've no intention of reacquainting myself with the joys now.'

Meaning I'm no major temptation! *Terrific!*

She was horrified to catch herself contemplating just how long it would take her to make Mr Iron Control Tyler eat his words...and maybe her too!

'I never have,' she revealed absently as she slipped off her jacket prior to pulling on the fleece.

'Never have what?' Quinn selected a few more items before zipping up the bag and flinging it over his head.

'Made out in a car,' she elaborated, pulling the top over her head. She smoothed down her ruffled hair and found that Quinn was looking at her with a startled expression.

'Never…?'

She shook her head.

'Your education really was neglected, love.'

The expression in his eyes was making her nervous. It might be her imagination, but to Rowena it suggested that Quinn wouldn't mind filling in the gaps in her education personally.

'It's hardly an obligatory development milestone and I had more important things than groping on my mind in my teens,' she told him with lofty scorn.

'Aren't you curious?'

'Not even slightly,' she said, clumsily drawing her padded jacket on over the fleece.

'Well, if you change your mind…'

Rowena flushed to the roots of her hair. Laughing to himself, Quinn began adding his own layers.

The sound of his deep laughter made her grit her teeth. In her line of work, Rowena had flirted with film stars and discussed the global economy with statesmen; she could hold her own in the most sophisticated of company and she didn't enjoy the novel experience of being made to feel like a gauche, inexperienced adolescent.

'Shall we pool our supplies?' Quinn asked once he was satisfied Rowena was insulated to his satisfaction, which involved the addition of several layers of unattractive clothing. He laid out two chocolate bars and a packet of mints on the dashboard. 'I suppose you're on a permanent diet.' He sounded resigned. 'Nothing remotely resembling carbohydrate or sugar in your pockets?'

'I don't diet, but neither do I fill my pockets with junk food on the off chance I get cut off by a blizzard.'

'Have you not got *anything* useful on your person?'

'Perhaps it would have been more sensible to ask me that before you made me pile on the layers. I feel like a mummy,' Rowena complained.

Head on one side, he considered her suggestion. 'Nah,' he denied. 'You look like one of those little nests of cute Russian dolls. What are they called…?'

'I'm not sure, but the way I recall it they don't have waists.' She glanced down at her own disguised by the bulk of her clothes and went a little paler as she remembered that her own would most likely be just a memory soon.

'No slur on your waistline intended,' he soothed, amused by this unusual display of feminine vanity. 'You know, I had a set of them when I was a kid. Removing the outer layers never lost its appeal for me…'

His indolent drawl, laced with sexual innuendo, had Rowena shivering under her layers and frantically breaking contact with those mesmeric eyes of his—eyes that carried a message not nearly as innocent as his words.

'I thought dolls were for girls,' she mocked, looking away, her cheeks self-consciously pink.

'My parents are the couple least likely to be heard saying boys will be boys. They were dead against sexual stereotyping of any type,' he explained solemnly. 'I was encouraged to be in touch with my feminine side from an early age, and I'd say,' he admitted with a provocative leer, 'that on the whole it paid dividends.'

'I doubt very much if your parents had those sort of dividends in mind,' she observed with a disgusted sniff.

'They could give you some lessons in not being narrow-minded,' he shot back.

'I'm not narrow-minded because I find your bed-hopping lifestyle distasteful,' she countered austerely.

A look of sardonic amusement gradually spread across his face as his green eyes searched her flushed features.

'You're jealous!' He laughed with throaty masculine delight.

Rowena's mouth was actually open to hotly deny this ridiculous claim when a thrill of shocked recognition shot through her body—he was right! The thought of Quinn with other women brought out the green-eyed monster in her.

'Nothing,' she lied shakily, 'could be farther from the truth. I don't envy your conquests, I just wish like hell I hadn't been one of them. In fact,' she added, warming to her theme, 'if I could go back and erase one moment in my life it would be that one in New York!'

She heard the hissing sound of Quinn's furious inhalation, deeply regretful of what she'd said and just as deeply determined not to retract it.

'And that would be because you hated every minute of it...?' With eyes like ice chips and a harsh, scathing frown on his face, Quinn still looked sinfully attractive—in fact, if she was totally honest, the menace added an element of not unattractive danger.

'Yes…no…you know I didn't. You're a perfect lover! Happy now?' she asked, her voice thick with resentment.

'Not especially. If it was so damned *perfect*, why do you want to erase it?'

Shaking her head, Rowena turned away from the simmering fury in his frustrated glare. Chin cupped in her hands, she rocked forward in her seat and sighed.

When she lifted her head Quinn was shocked to see the sparkle of tears on the end of her long eyelashes.

'If it hadn't happened my life wouldn't be so complicated.'

Quinn gave a snort of disgust. 'What is it with you? Don't you allow for *any* spontaneity at all in your life?'

His easy contempt brought all her fear and resentment rushing to the surface. How easy it was for him, how simple—he wasn't the one carrying a baby; he wasn't the one whose life had jumped about a hundred scary miles off track!

'I have no intention of making excuses for the way I am to you or anybody else, and I don't share your fondness for spontaneity,

Quinn, which is hardly surprising. If I hadn't been so *spontaneous* I wouldn't be pregnant!' she yelled.

There was a delay of perhaps twenty seconds before Quinn's head went back as though she'd landed a blow on his jaw—or maybe somewhere even more sensitive. Clamping a hand over her mouth, she watched the healthy colour seep from his face until his bronzed skin looked almost greyish.

Rowena's own colour wasn't looking too healthy. Saying it out loud had suddenly made the pregnancy scarily real; until this moment she'd been able to file the facts away for future consideration. That was no longer possible; the situation had suddenly been catapulted into the here and now!

'Oh, God! I didn't mean to blurt it out like that…' Was there a gentle way of telling someone he was going to be a father? 'But you made me so angry…'

Looking curiously vacant, Quinn's glazed sea-green eyes fixed frowningly on her face. *'Pregnant…?'* He caught his breath in a long sibilant hiss. 'You did say pregnant…? With *my* baby?'

Rowena flinched. The question hurt her more than she had thought possible.

'Sorry, but there are no other candidates.' She rubbed a shaky, distracted hand over her forehead and felt the clammy dampness of her skin. She shook her head. 'Forget I said anything,' she instructed him with a bitter little laugh. 'This is my problem.'

'Forget!'

Rowena could almost feel the waves of incredulous fury emanating from his rigid frame.

'So this is why you've been avoiding me. This is why you wouldn't speak to me... When were you going to tell me?' His eyes narrowed. 'Or *weren't* you going to tell me...?'

This was just the start! Rowena shook her head and closed her eyes, envisaging the inevitable recriminations, arguments and ultimatums, and the unstable concoction of fear, hurt and unacknowledged yearning that she'd been keeping a lid on over the past few weeks suddenly exploded.

Tears began to cascade silently down her alabaster-pale cheeks until with a husky cry she tore open the car door and, oblivious to Quinn's harsh warning cries, she stepped out into the darkness. It didn't matter that she had nowhere to run to—the instinct to run away went beyond logic.

Actually it was more a matter of stumbling than running. The snow was still falling in a blinding horizontal sheet and it was lying a good two feet deep on the ground—considerably deeper where it had drifted. The world was white on black, but not silent black or still white, but a noisy, roaring, inhospitable place that filled her ears with a constant howl and almost drowned out the thunderous thump of her own heartbeat. She struggled onwards, her head bowed against the biting intensity of the driving snow, which bit into her skin like sharp ice pellets.

Rowena concentrated on her feet, picking them up one at a time, and taking the next step. If she thought at all it was just about keeping going and picking herself up when she stumbled.

The picking herself up part rapidly became more and more difficult. When it came to the point where every step was agony and each breath made her feel as if her lungs were on fire, perhaps someone with less guts and sheer pigheaded stubbornness would have lain down quietly in the soft snow, but it didn't occur to Rowena even for one second to give up—she was not one of life's quitters.

The dry stone wall she encountered suddenly offered a little respite from the worst of the wind. She squatted down behind it trying to catch her breath and pondering glumly on the reckless stupidity of her actions. The logic that had told her escaping from the safety of the car was a really good idea was growing fuzzier by the second.

Now she had the leisure to think, it finally dawned on her that she was in very real danger. The chain of events that had led her, the accomplished editor of a world-famous magazine, to this place was of secondary importance. What she needed to focus her thoughts on was getting herself back to the car.

Where was the car?

She gulped and pushed aside the gibbering fear that was just a whisper away. She'd done the wrong thing; now it was time to do the right thing. There was a right thing to do in the circumstances, *wasn't there*...?

Her racing brain retrieved the useful memory of a documentary she'd recently watched about people who'd survived in far worse situations than this. The tale of a chap who had survived for three nights in sub-zero temperatures on Snowdonia had featured prominently. Of course, she was neither well equipped nor an ex-SAS member, which made the link tenuous—but how hard could it be to dig a hole in the snow and sit tight…? She shivered and wished she'd paid more attention to the survival details they'd described at the time.

Noticing that the blackness around was less dense, she stood up and, braving the worst of the buffeting chilly wind, scanned the bleak landscape for some clue as to which way she'd come, or some sign of life, a house…*anything*! She was about to sink back down, her spirits rock-bottom, when she caught a glimpse of movement.

Heart racing hopefully, she lifted a hand to shield her eyes and squinted through the blizzard. She gave a sob of relief as she made out the definite outline of a tall figure moving parallel to her. It was impossible to make out any details but Rowena was sure it was Quinn; it had to be Quinn.

Rowena saw no conflict between her craving to find a safe haven in Quinn's arms and her recent, equally strong desire to flee from him. *He's coming for me.*

Her blissful anticipation of rescue was short-lived. It didn't take her long to figure out that if he carried on in that direction he'd not see her at all. The situation called for immediate action.

She leapt to her feet, waving her warms above her head. Her cries were whipped away by the wind. The solitary figure, battling through the elements on the course that would take him away from her, remained oblivious to her wild gesticulations and cries.

She had to get to him.

The burst of adrenaline that surged through her body enabled her to keep going longer than would otherwise have been possible, but eventually not even Rowena's legendary determination could keep her on her feet.

Lying face down in the snow, so exhausted she couldn't lift a finger, Rowena felt the tears seep from between her closed eyelids and for the first time in her life contemplated defeat.

The tears hadn't been flowing very long when she felt a large hand clamp over her shoulder. A moment later she was hauled bodily to her feet.

Big, capable gloved hands cupped her face and brushed the snow from it. Rowena found herself looking into a grim face that looked harsh enough to be carved from the savage elements. Snow clung to Quinn's long eyelashes and dark brows, his skin looked especially dark in contrast, and his sea-green eyes glittered like gems.

'Quinn,' she mouthed weakly, but nothing audible emerged as her lips moved stiffly. Closing her eyes, she let her body sag limply against him. She felt his chest lift as a powerful sigh juddered through his body, then his arms closed tightly about her. For a moment they stood that way, his breath warm against her cheek as her heartbeat slowed to a frantic canter.

For a short, blissful time Rowena completely forgot the storm raging around them.

Too soon he was pushing her away and his keen gaze was skimming urgently over her face as his hands moved in a similarly capable, clinical manner over her body, checking for injuries. He couldn't see any signs of injury, but… 'Are you hurt?'

Rowena sensed his bellowed question rather than heard it as his words were snatched away by an extra-strong gust of wind. It was crazy, she reflected. Nothing essentially had changed about her situation, it was still fraught with danger—danger of her own making! Even a man like Quinn, who only saw problems as things to be solved rather than insurmountable obstacles, couldn't subdue the elements, but somehow his mere presence made a positive outcome to the situation seem inevitable.

Quinn saw her shake her head to indicate her unharmed condition, and relief more intense than anything he had ever felt before flooded through him. She was all right—he could afford to be angry now.

Rowena recoiled from the lick of fury in his eyes.

'Have your lost your mind, woman?' he asked with hoarse incredulity.

Better lose my mind than my heart, she thought glumly.

'How far is the car?' As her own stupidity was not something she could defend it seemed appropriate to change the subject.

Quinn frowned and brought his face down to level with hers. His nose nudged hers and she felt his exhaled breath warm on her icily numb face. She repeated her question.

'Not far—and I've an excellent sense of direction,' he replied. There was little point panicking her. He'd been too busy concentrating on following Rowena's tracks in the snow, which were being covered at a terrifyingly rapid rate, to look out for landmarks.

'That means you've no idea either,' she translated. 'Aren't you supposed to be desperately woodsy? What about those back-to-nature stints you were always taking—communing with nature and all that rubbish?'

Quinn didn't reply. He just turned up the fur-trimmed collar of her jacket and, taking her face firmly between his hands, kissed her hard on the lips.

His lips have to be cold, so mine must be colder, Rowena surmised vaguely as his warm mouth moved in a very expert fashion against her own lips, which parted easily under his probing assault. His thrusting tongue hungrily sought the deep recesses of her open mouth and the warm, lethargic feeling that had spread through her treacherously co-operative body morphed into hot, liquid fire. With a throaty cry she pressed her supple body up against him and moulded herself to the hard, inflexible contours of his male body.

A small moan of protest emerged from her lips when he stopped kissing her and lifted his head.

'My God, woman, but you do choose your moments!' Quinn breathed, a wry smile tugging at one corner of his mouth.

'You started it.' And finished it! She cleared her throat, embarrassed by the recognition that she'd displayed considerably less will-power than him.

After a brief glance into her antagonistic face Quinn pulled the thermal-lined leather gloves off his own hands and slid them onto her icy extremities.

Her mouth opened in protest. 'But...'

'For once in your life, shut up!' he advised, giving her collar a final tweak.

Rowena was still in a submissively shocked, post-kiss condition when he heaved all five feet ten of her casually across his shoulder, fireman fashion, and strode off.

'Comfy?' he bellowed over his shoulder.

'No!' Rowena hit his broad back with her fists a couple of times and yelled insults about Neanderthals, but it was a purely token protest. It might be a very ungainly form of transport, but she was too exhausted to raise any serious objections to this treatment.

Fortunately there was nobody about to see her ignominious position, for if there had been her credibility as a serious feminist would have been shot to hell! She settled herself into as comfortable a position as was possible and comforted herself with the fact she could blame any future kissing incidents on the prolonged rush of blood to the head she was experiencing.

Quinn soon realised that the odds on them finding their way back to the car were remote. His eyes methodically scanned the horizon, searching for some form of shelter as he tramped carefully onward. His thoughts were growing grim when he caught his first glimpse of the chimney stack just visible behind the copse of trees. He judged it couldn't be more than a hundred metres or so away.

Rowena felt him pause and change direction. She lifted her head.

'What is it?' she mouthed, craning her head around at an angle to get a glimpse of his profile.

Rowena followed the direction of his gaze when he jerked his head in the direction of the dark patch of skeletal trees up ahead. She couldn't see anything, but Quinn obviously could and she was prepared to take it on faith; Quinn wasn't the type to hallucinate. She mimed her desire to get down and after a moment he acquiesced.

With his arm around her waist hugging her to his side, they made their way towards the small copse. It felt to Rowena as if it took for ever, but eventually they reached a small rusty gate that led up what, before the snow, might have been a garden path to the front door of the stone cottage that the chimney stack was attached to.

By this time it was slightly more morning than night, and the pale grey dawn light made it easier to assess their surroundings. Quinn pulled the hood back from his head and scanned the unfriendly aspect of the building.

Rowena did the same, displaying far less objectivity about the closed and deserted look of the house than he was. 'It doesn't look as if anyone's at home,' she quavered as her heart sank. Her spirits lifted a little as she recalled the uncivilised hour. 'But they'd be in bed, wouldn't they?'

'Possibly,' Quinn agreed, sparing her the briefest of glances. 'If so we're about to wake them up.' He manoeuvred his way past a snow-covered garden trough filled with ice-encrusted Christmas roses and hammered on the front door.

There was no reply.

'Stop there. I'll go and check around the back.' His perceptive glance swivelled back to her face. 'You got a problem with that?'

Rowena closed her mouth and swallowed back the instinctive protest on her tongue. She shook her head firmly as if the idea of being left alone didn't make her as jumpy as hell. Her chin went up.

'I'll be fine.'

'Good girl,' he approved, his eyes crinkling deliciously as he smiled warmly at her.

She watched worriedly as he edged his way around the far corner of the building. His shoulder caught the branch of a snow-laden tree and dumped its entire covering onto the ground, almost blocking the path he'd just taken.

She stamped her feet on the ground. They'd be really painful when the circulation began to return—*if* it ever began to return. No, cancel the *if*. Be positive, Rowena! Quinn was probably not gone much more than five minutes, but to Rowena it felt like a lot longer.

When she heard the unmistakable sounds of the bolts on the front door being pushed back she smiled from pure, delirious relief and rubbed her gloved hands together in eager anticipation.

When the door swung inwards the heavy snow lying against it fell inside the room with a rush. Quinn appeared.

'Someone was in,' she cried, standing back while he kicked some of the powdery snow back outside.

'No.'

'No?' A frown creased the smoothness of her wide brow 'Then how…?' A hand shot out and pulled her unceremonially inside.

Rubbing her arm, Rowena glared at Quinn as he closed the door against the elements. 'I broke in,' he explained, turning back to her once the process was completed.

Rowena's eyes widened. 'B-but you can't just *break in*…' she stuttered, her law-abiding instincts deeply shocked by his casual disclosure. She blinked as he shone a torch across her face.

'There's no electricity but I found this. Take it,' he added, pushing a second torch into her hands.

'You stole it.'

'If you're going to be pedantic, I borrowed it,' he responded in reply to her disapproving retort. 'What would you suggest we do, Rowena?' Quinn asked, sounding exasperated. 'Stumble around in the dark, or maybe freeze to death outside?'

'No, of course not, but—'

'No buts about it,' Quinn retorted, handing her the torch and turning to pull open a heavy curtain from a window.'

'Heavens!' Rowena exclaimed, taking note of the room she was standing in for the first time.

'Yeah, not what you expect, is it?'

It certainly wasn't. The modest exterior of the building gave little hint of the fact that the inside of what must originally have been a pretty humble cottage had been virtually ripped out to leave one large open-plan living area on the ground floor. The flagstone floors were scattered with a selection of good quality, bright ethnic rugs. The original artwork on the stone walls was equally colourful and the eclectic mixture of furniture shrieked expensive.

'I wonder who lives here?'

'Well, whoever does, they weren't expecting visitors.'

Rowena responded with automatic antagonism to his authoritative tone. 'How do you know?'

'Only one bed.' He nodded towards the polished wood staircase that led upstairs. 'A big bed,' he added, a definite note of amused approval in his voice.

'How can you think about beds at a time like this?' she asked, trying hard not to let her mind dwell on the joint subject of Quinn and large beds.

'I was thinking of the lack of spare beds—not what goes on in them.'

I wasn't, Rowena admitted to herself.

Shivering, she continued to examine their surroundings while Quinn began to open up the rest of the curtains. The south-facing wall of the room turned out to be almost totally glass, and it had the effect of bringing the outdoors into the room. Rowena could see how that might be rather nice on a sunlit evening, or even on a terrible snowy evening if the heating was on full blast and there was a big fire in the hearth, but right now it made her shiver uncontrollably and look away. It was hard not to think about what might have been if Quinn hadn't found her.

Quinn looked around, mentally prioritising. For the moment personal interests had to be of secondary importance. 'It could be worse,' he conceded, rubbing his hands together. 'Next…a bit of heat, I think,' he decided after a moment's practical reflection.

He opened the doors of the black cast-iron wood burner that sat in the big stone inglenook and found it laid ready to light. Another quick search revealed a convenient box of matches on top of the log basket on the hearth. He waited until the tinder inside caught and closed the door and turned to Rowena.

'We can't just make ourselves at home, Quinn,' Rowena fretted.

'If it makes you any happier you can make a full inventory of any items we use and we can leave our phone numbers. You could start now—item one, two matches…'

'I suppose…' she began dubiously.

Quinn's dark brows slated satirically. 'I was joking.'

'Well, I'm not, and what if the owners come home and find us…squatting?' Unable to stop shivering violently, Rowena moved closer to the giant room heater, which was beginning to chuck out a little warmth—just enough to stop her breath freezing quite so obviously in the air.

'That's hardly likely, given the weather conditions, but if they do it'll save me the bother of finding the fuse box. Not that it's likely to help. I suspect we can put the lack of power down to a localised cut. Or maybe not so local,' he mused thoughtfully. 'The snow's probably brought half the lines in the county down.'

Rowena searched his face and found no signs of the guilty discomfort she was experiencing. She found it incredible he could just walk into someone else's home and not feel like a thief, and she envied him.

'Doesn't it bother you *at all* that we're breaking and entering?'

'I'd prefer to see myself featured in the tabloids as a daring housebreaker than a frozen corpse,' he admitted frankly.

When it was put like that, her concerns did seem trivial.

'Which reminds me…' Rowena watched as his dark glossy head bent. He began systematically opening the doors of the handsome maple kitchen cupboards until, with a grunt of triumph, he emerged with a thick piece of card, which after a bit of judicious trimming he proceeded to jam in the hole in the window he had smashed to get inside.

Rowena smiled reluctantly as she slowly stretched her aching limbs. No number of hours dutifully—some would say obsessively—spent in the gym had prepared her well-toned thigh and calf muscles for tramping through snow. 'Are you sure you haven't done this before?'

Quinn turned, his narrowed eyes focusing on her face. 'Today's just full of firsts…' he revealed unsmilingly.

It wasn't hard to catch his drift. Rowena's breath escaped in one long silent hiss, her hands curled tightly inside the too-big gloves as she tensed expectantly, but to her relief he didn't pursue the subject.

'I don't suppose that jacket is waterproof?'

'Maybe not, but it's in this season's *must have* colour…' she explained, tongue firmly in cheek. 'Do you like it? I got my usual thirty per cent discount…'

Quinn liked what was in it. 'Nice to see you haven't lost your sense of humour.'

'I didn't think you thought I had one.' She stopped, shaking too hard to continue.

Quinn silently berated himself for standing around chatting while she was freezing. 'You must be wet to the skin,' he announced after subjecting her dejected figure to a searching scrutiny. 'We need to get you out of them and into dry things,' he said, concern in his eyes despite his brusque tone. 'Pity there's no hot water. What you could do with is a really hot bath…' His voice trailed off.

Despite the fact Quinn was an exceptionally disciplined man and he knew his main priority was doing everything within his means to ensure their survival, he couldn't evict a maverick image from his mind of the long hot steamy bath they'd shared that night in his hotel room in New York.

It took all his will-power to finally dispel the image of Rowena, her sultry smile just about visible through the wet strands of hair plastered across her face the moment before she'd thrown her head back and stretched her arms languorously above her head. The action had drawn her firm breasts upwards as he'd allowed the water cupped in his hands to slowly fall over the rosy-tipped quivering peaks.

'Quinn…Quinn…are you all right?'

The odd glazed expression slid from his eyes as he gave his head a tiny shake and focused on Rowena's concerned face.

'Did you say something?' he said, sounding unaccountably defensive to Rowena.

Her puzzled frown deepened. 'Are you all right?'

'Barring the odd touch of frostbite—' he extended his hands palm up towards her '—I'm fine.'

She stopped puzzling over the unusually harsh rasp in his voice as she examined his tapering fingertips. It wasn't just the thought of those clever fingers being harmed that made her stomach muscles quiver violently.

'Don't joke about it,' she pleaded huskily, touching the tip of her tongue to the beads of moisture along her upper lip.

'Sit by the fire and get some of those wet things off. I'll go upstairs and see what I can…*borrow*.' One brow arched, he shot her a challenging look.

Rowena shrugged her shoulders and threw him the torch she still carried.

Once she was alone she did as Quinn requested, though unfastening buttons was not easy with fingers that were slow and clumsy with cold. She had stripped down to her bra, pants, shirt and socks by the time he returned.

Quinn returned quietly. The hunched figure, her slender back turned to him, was violently shivering before the fire. He was engulfed by a wave of tenderness so intense it felt as if a hand had casually thrust through his ribs and were squeezing his heart.

It was the sound of Quinn's soft, sibilant curse that made Rowena conscious she was no longer alone. Like a startled animal she turned her head and their eyes meshed, violet blue with deep green. No glare of oncoming headlights could have been as paralysing as his intense scrutiny, nor could they have made her feel more helpless and vulnerable.

'What's wrong?' she asked.

As questions went that one was particularly dumb, and his tight-lipped grim response underlined the dumbness. 'How long have you got?'

Rowena bit her lip and turned her head away.

She dealt on a daily basis with important, powerful people and she had never been short of a clever reply. Quinn was the only person she knew who could make her feel stupid, clumsy and totally inadequate. This alone was reason enough not to get involved with him. Pity I didn't figure that out a bit sooner, she reflected, pushing aside the memories still fresh in her mind that completely contradicted this bitter theory. The flip side of feeling stupid and clumsy was feeling gloriously empowered and energised—embracing your sexuality was a scary thing to do at her age!

She watched as he dropped the large pile of stuff he was carrying on the nearest armchair and advanced towards her carrying a white fluffy bath sheet, which he draped around her from head to toe.

Rowena felt the blast of heat as he opened the wood burner with the toe of his boot and threw on a couple more dry logs, which immediately began to crackle satisfactorily. Quinn then threw off his own waterproof, which, unlike her own, seemed to have lived up to its description before he joined her.

'Now let's get your circulation moving,' he said, dropping down onto his knees in front of her. 'You look blue,' he added, swallowing hard as his eyes scanned the slender rounded contours of her long slim legs.

'W…what are you doing?' Wobbling, she leant heavily on his shoulder as he lifted one foot to roll down her sodden sock. It hit the floor with a wet thwack as he tossed it carelessly over his shoulder.

'You're so untidy,' she disapproved as he allowed her to replace her bare foot on the ground. 'Show a bit of respect—this is someone else's home.'

Quinn lifted his head and looked around the big living space. 'I don't know,' he mused. 'I think I could feel at home here.'

'I thought you already did. I'd feel a lot happier if you didn't.' She couldn't throw off the guilty conviction that any minute now the real owners would walk through the door.

'We'll debate the moral aspects later,' he promised drily as the other sock joined its mate. 'I'd prefer to concentrate my efforts on avoiding hypothermia right now, if you don't mind. Take that shirt off,' he instructed her tersely. 'And whatever's underneath it.'

The last time Quinn had ordered her to remove intimate items of her clothing there had been a lot less objectivity in his manner. Rowena dismissed this memory, ashamed of the rush of heat it brought to the surface of her cold skin and the achy quivering effect low in her belly.

Irrationally she even found herself resenting his practicality. Perhaps now he knew she was pregnant he didn't think of her in *that* way…? This was a definite possibility—after all, how many men found hugely pregnant women seductive…? Rowena didn't know, but she suspected most who claimed they did were just paying lip-service.

She could always ignore his instruction on principle—the principle being what, exactly, Rowena? she asked herself mockingly. What's bothering me anyhow? If she had an ounce of common sense she'd be thanking her lucky stars that exposure to low temperatures and the thought of her shortly being the size of an elephant made him immune to her charms!

'Don't just stand there, woman, it's not like I haven't seen everything there is to see,' he reminded her crudely.

'The last time you were invited.' She immediately regretted introducing this subject as an image floated before her eyes of herself with her skirt yanked up around the top of her thighs, her shirt open to the waist revealing shamelessly swollen nipples still glistening and wet from the ministrations of his tongue and lips as she lay beneath him, begging him with hoarse urgency to do whatever he liked—and as quickly as possible! Dry-throated, she swallowed. The shame and, worse still, the fizz of hot squirmy excitement low in her belly made her assiduously avoid his eyes.

She still couldn't believe it had been her doing and saying those things. Through the concealing shield of her lashes she saw his dark head lift once more.

'So I was…' The smoky reflective gleam in his eyes made Rowena, whose heart was already banging frantically against her ribcage, wonder if he was recalling the same moment—mind you, there had been others equally incriminating. One corner of his mobile mouth lifted in his trade-mark lazy half-smile. 'If it makes you happier I won't peek.'

Rowena had no intention of giving him the opportunity!

Careful not to dislodge the concealing bath sheet, she slid her arms out of the shirt and slipped it over her narrow shoulders, very conscious that all she now wore were her bra and an insubstantial pair of pants.

It occurred to her as she modestly unclipped her light lacy bra in a similar fashion that she was behaving in a totally untypical coy fashion—it wasn't her own body she wasn't comfortable with, but the way Quinn made her feel about that body. Unlike any other man of her acquaintance he made her feel like a deeply sexual woman, a woman with strong appetites and uncontrollable passions. She didn't think she knew that woman very well—she trusted her even less!

Quinn made no comment, but she could almost hear his sarcastic thoughts when she folded both items of clothing into a neat parcel before disposing of them.

'Ouch, that hurts!' she protested as he began to rub her legs briskly with a second towel.

Tingling life painfully returned to her limbs as he ignored her protests.

'Don't be a baby!' His curt tone was as abrasive as his actions.

She felt his rhythmic actions falter at just about the same moment the 'B' word made the inevitable link in her own head too. He looked awfully pale—perhaps he was in denial as she had been at first...?

Lower lip caught between her teeth—it stopped it trembling—and still tented in the bath sheet, she took the other towel from his hands.

The atmosphere of slightly uneasy intimacy had become one of cold suspicion and hostility.

'You don't need a medical diploma on the wall to do that, I think I can manage now,' she mumbled, avoiding his eyes.

After a moment Quinn released the towel with a curt nod.

'If that's what you want. Only it's not going to go away, Rowena.' She didn't make the mistake of thinking he was referring to her goose-bumps. 'Unless of course you make it go away...?'

CHAPTER FIVE

THE full significance of Quinn's tense postscript was lost on Rowena for a full twenty seconds. When his meaning did finally hit her, her violet-blue eyes shot open.

'You think that I'd...?' Drawing herself up to her full height, she fixed her outraged gaze coldly on the man still kneeling at her feet.

Despite his stance there was nothing remotely submissive about Quinn's expression. Neither, much to her amazement, did it contain any of the critical condemnation she'd expected to see. Her righteous wrath fizzled away as she recognised the tense apprehension in his unblinking emerald stare.

Apprehension wasn't something she associated with Quinn. He always gave the impression of being so completely in control of himself and events, but he was undoubtedly stealing himself to hear her reply. What did you expect? she derided herself scornfully. You told the man you were carrying his baby just before you ran off into a blizzard forcing him to risk life and limb to save you. You didn't have to be very imaginative to figure out these events might have shaken even Quinn's impregnable self-assurance.

The hypocrisy of her own outraged posture also struck her forcibly—why *wouldn't* he think she'd consider the easy option? It was only when she had considered it that she herself had realised that abortion was *not* an easy option—not for her at least…

She heaved a tiny sigh and shook her head—the gesture was infinitesimal, but it had a dramatic effect on Quinn, who visibly slumped with relief as the tension eased from his lean body. Quinn's eyes closed. He pressed the heel of his hand to his forehead and massaged the tightly stretched skin, then exhaled heavily.

His eyes opened.

'I'm glad.'

This throaty revelation was unnecessary—Rowena had never seen anything that approached the concentrated elation she saw briefly reflected in his gleaming eyes.

Pressing his hands against his well-muscled thighs, he then rose in one smooth, supple motion. Just watching him move made her tummy muscles clench rhythmically. Without speaking, he caught the edges of the towel draped over her shoulders, pulled it up over her head and began to systematically blot the moisture from her hair.

Rowena stood there meekly accepting his ministrations, fighting the ridiculous urge to turn her face into his capacious palm and press her lips against his warm skin, and wondering with the tiny remaining sane portion of her mind why he wasn't saying anything else—he had to want to.

She broke the silence when she could no longer stand wondering.

'Don't get the idea…I mean…this isn't an unplanned teenage pregnancy…'

His slanted satirical smile didn't reach his watchful eyes. 'Is there something you're not telling me?'

'I meant the teenage part,' she elaborated swiftly, horrified that he might think even for one minute she'd got pregnant deliberately. 'It's not like I didn't know all the options open to me.' Sure, the sarcastic voice in her head agreed, you were so clued up you didn't even protect yourself properly. 'And I did think about it…*not* having the baby,' she admitted, a shade of defensiveness creeping into her tone as her heavy lashes lifted off her cheek.

Quinn's eyes flickered briefly down to hers before he returned his attention to his task.

'Considering the number of times you've lectured me on the rights a woman should have over her own body, this doesn't come as a massive shock. But you've made your decision...'

Rowena's eyes widened—he was right, it was time to throw the pro and con lists she'd religiously compiled out of the window. She'd have saved a lot of time if she'd just followed her gut instincts from the beginning.

'That's the important thing.'

'It was my decision to make.' It seemed critical to establish this.

'Yes.'

Perversely his ready compliance annoyed her. Anyone would think she wanted him to give her an argument, call her a shallow ice-maiden who put her career before everything else. Maybe deep down she thought she deserved condemnation.

'And I suppose you expect me to believe you'd be displaying this impressive tolerance and understanding if my decision didn't happen to be the one you wanted me to make?' Or was she making yet another assumption...? Maybe the thought of fatherhood under these circumstances didn't please him—maybe he totally hated the idea...? Perhaps he'd like nothing better than to learn she was planning an abortion...? There was a big difference between wanting to share a bed with an independent woman and being lumbered with the responsibilities of fatherhood.

Rowena had heard enough horror stories to know that even when the event was planned a baby could put the most stable relationship under a lot of strain. This didn't surprise her, but what did was the fact that most of these people reduced to walking zombies by their newborn offspring frequently went on to have another baby and in some cases more than that!

Not that it was reasonable to compare herself and Quinn to these people. By no stretch of the imagination could what they had be termed stable—for that matter it could hardly be termed a relationship!

Quinn's eyes skimmed her face, acknowledging her cynical, slightly wary expression with a wry grimace. Heaving a sigh, he let the towel slide back down to her shoulders and finally stopped acting as if extracting every last drop of moisture from her hair was all he was thinking about.

'I could say I'm the very epitome of liberal-minded political correctness...but I'm not an impartial observer here, Rowena. There would have been some...conflict,' he admitted, choosing his words with obvious care.

'Meaning you'd have fought me every inch of the way,' Rowena translated, feeling foolishly relieved to know he wouldn't prefer her to get rid of the baby.

'Meaning I'd have done what I had to. I respect the fact it's your body and therefore the ultimate decision has to be yours, but it's *our* baby and I'd have done my utmost—not just because of the baby, but because...' He stopped mid impassioned speech and surveyed her face with darkened eyes. 'I don't think any of us know how we're going to act in a given situation until we find ourselves there.'

Rowena relaxed a little and nodded. She didn't resent his truthfulness. Honesty always had been one of Quinn's most attractive characteristics—if you left out the incredible body, the air of attractive danger and a voice that could soften the most cynical female, deep inside where it mattered.

'Sometimes,' she admitted huskily, matching his honesty with some of her own, 'things seem all right, in theory...' Her expression grew sombre as she contemplated with trepidation the inevitable long-reaching consequences this decision was going to have on her life and future.

'Admitting you are wrong isn't a sign of weakness.'

Her indignation flared—as if he was the expert on admitting he was wrong! 'What are you doing?' she gasped as, totally without warning, Quinn swept her up into his arms.

Alarming as it was to find herself cradled in extremely strong masculine arms, when you were five feet ten inches there was some novelty value in being treated as if you weighed nothing. She recalled how far he'd carried her earlier in the blizzard and realised with a tinge of awe that his impressive physique was not just for show. Rowena was just beginning to almost enjoy herself when Quinn spoiled it.

'You're really not as light as you look.' He grunted as he hefted her a little higher into his arms.

Rowena scowled at his hawkish profile as she automatically threw an arm over his shoulder to steady herself. Just because she had never felt the urge to seek shelter in strong male arms, it didn't mean she relished being reminded she wasn't one of those petite females who brought out the protective, chivalrous instincts in men. On the other hand, men—the ones she didn't intimidate—saw her as a challenge, someone to be subdued.

'Nobody asked you to pick me up,' she reminded him sourly.

'It's quicker this way. We need to speed up the process—you're not warming up fast enough.'

Rowena had no argument with that—she felt as if she'd never be warm again—it was Quinn's method of achieving this desirable goal that had her worried. 'Will you put me down?'

Again with no warning he did as she requested, right onto the centrally situated, oversized sofa, which was laden with cushions and draped with a richly coloured kelim. Quinn impatiently brushed half the cushions onto the floor with his forearm and pushed the rest into a soft pile behind her back as he set her down. He then proceeded to drag the heavy sofa with her on it closer to the fire.

Before she could comment, let alone protest, he pulled a king-sized duvet from the stack of things he'd brought downstairs and with a curt instruction to, 'Lift your bottom, sweetheart!'

he slid it under her on the sofa, then folded it envelope-style over her.

Still shaking helplessly with cold that seemed to have bitten deep into her bones, she pushed her chin on top of the soft cocoon. 'Is it just with me you act like some sort of prehistoric caveman? Or don't you ever consult anybody…?'

She stopped and tried not to stare too obviously as Quinn began to unzip the leather trousers he was still wearing. She tried to be objective about what was revealed by his impromptu striptease, but it wasn't easy. He really had the very best legs a man could have, she decided, trying to drag her covetous gaze from the athletically bronzed strength of his long lower limbs.

'I'm sure consultation is a good thing and as a rule I'm all for it,' he asserted, acting as if he hadn't heard her loud sceptical snort. 'But when a problem needs to be resolved without delay I don't think committee decisions are the most effective way of going about it.'

'I always had you pegged as one of those despotic types in a previous life,' she revealed crankily. If he shed his clothes half as fast as he made decisions she didn't have long before she was in deep trouble. Rowena despised her weakness as the heavy dragging sensation low in her pelvis got increasingly difficult to ignore.

'A benevolent despot.'

'There's no such thing,' she claimed throatily.

'Remember when I mentioned the skin-to-skin way of raising body temperature?'

Rowena gulped—as if she could have forgotten. A wave of faintness made her head spin as she contemplated what he appeared to be suggesting.

'Well, this is a modified version.' Hand extended, he passed her the fine woollen top he'd been wearing next to his skin.

Rowena tore her gaze from his lean, finely muscled torso and looked at it blankly, her eyes huge in her pale face.

'It's warm; put it on,' he urged.

Warm from his skin, which at the moment was only covered by a pair of designer boxers! Her nipples, perhaps in anticipation of the second-hand warmth on offer, began to tingle and harden into tight, painful buds—heaven knew what they'd do if it was firsthand warmth!

'It won't bite.'

Rowena wished she shared his confidence, not to mention his clinical objectivity. If she could have thought of one sensible reason why she shouldn't lay material still warm from his skin against her own, Rowena would have used it to avoid a gesture of such unavoidable intimacy.

Her fevered mind couldn't come up with an even semi-sensible reason so, nodding, she took a deep breath and forced her clenched fingers to unlock. Holding the quilt in her teeth, she eased her hand out from beneath the cover and snatched the top from him. Ducking down under the folds, she pulled the top over her head, the soft material chafing against her oversensitised breasts as she eased her arms into the sleeves. He was right—it was still warm with his body heat.

When she emerged her overbright eyes discovered Quinn was pushing his own arms back into one of his outer layers—a black fleece slightly thicker than the one he'd handed her.

'I wouldn't have looked.'

Two red circles appeared on her pale cheeks. 'I prefer not to take any chances.'

He eyed the hostile tilt of her chin and his big shoulders lifted in a surprisingly good-natured shrug. 'You're probably right,' he conceded as he approached the sofa. 'Now budge over.'

Rowena's hands came up in a protective gesture across her chest that caused the quilt to slither down to her waist. Hastily she snatched it up again. *'What?* You can't… you're not…'

Rowena discovered almost immediately that he could and was!

She closed her eyes and held her body rigid as his long, lean body slid under the cover and lay down beside her. The duvet settled back around them.

'Phase two…'

'Oh, no!' she whimpered under her breath. 'This really isn't what I want,' she added in a firmer tone. She was confident that Quinn wasn't the sort of man who would cross that particular line even if he thought she was lying through her teeth. If he responds with a corny, You don't know what you want, I'll kill him, Rowena decided wrathfully—even if it is true.

Quinn slid onto his back. 'Lie on top of me.'

'No way!' After her extraordinarily submissive behaviour in New York, perhaps it wasn't so surprising that he had got the idea she liked being told what to do in bed—not that this brusque instruction bore any real resemblance to the huskily erotic requests he had made of her that night. Just thinking about the velvet

rasp in his voice sent shiver after voluptuous shiver down her rigid, trembling spine.

Quinn looked into her eyes and was worried by the glazed expression he saw there—hopefully nothing more sinister than exhaustion had put it there.

'God, you're shaking like a leaf. This is stupid, Rowena.'

'I'll warm up in a minute,' she said, not really believing it by this point.

'No, you won't. I'd offer to go on top, but I thought you'd prefer to be in control…'

Rowena couldn't smile at his joke; she was fast coming round to thinking that any control she had around Quinn could only ever be illusionary, and if he made the slightest move to touch her he'd know it too!

'Hell, woman, this isn't some elaborate seduction technique—you're suffering from mild hypothermia.' His expression grew grim as he thanked his lucky stars once more they'd found shelter when they had.

'I am?'

'Trust me, I'm a doctor…'

'Not my doctor.' Her doctor didn't make house calls wearing a skimpy pair of boxer shorts.

And thank god for that! The friendship barrier had been hard enough to get by without that added complication.

'And doctors are having their socks sued off by dissatisfied customers every day of the week,' she reminded him grouchily through chattering teeth.

'I'm not joking, Rowena, this is the most efficient way of raising your body temperature to a safe level.'

He was relieved to see that his words seemed to have finally convinced her that he wasn't joking about the urgency of the situation. All—all!—he had to do now was retain the sort of professional objectivity he had boasted he possessed.

She shot him a wary look. 'How do we do this?'

'However you like.' Whichever way it was going to hurt, of that he had no doubt. He'd spent the last couple of months in an almost constant state of arousal, fantasising like a teenager about her, and now she was about to press that much-fantasised-about flesh against his own and the only thing he was allowed to display was clinical objectivity. It didn't get much more painful than that!

He willed his uncooperative body to relax as Rowena cautiously slid a leg over his hips. Quinn smiled encouragingly and hoped the intense strain he felt didn't show as she placed a hand beside his shoulder. Nostrils flared, he averted his eyes from the pleasing movement of her breasts swinging free beneath her borrowed top. Miraculously his own body stayed inert as the rest of her celestial body—hell, he *loved* the long, lean elegant lines of her supple body—followed.

He shook his head and regretfully dispelled the sensual image from his head. He couldn't afford that indulgence—it was taking all his concentration and will-power to keep his natural bodily responses in check. Silently he began to recite the nerve supply to the entire gastro-intestinal tract. It was a technique he'd not employed for a long time, but it had worked when he was an inexperienced—in every sense of the word—student with a desire to please his first lover!

Rowena tried telling herself she was lying on top of a heat source, not a stunningly virile male in peak condition, but somehow she couldn't visualise Quinn as a hot-water bottle! She bit down so hard on her lower lip to stop herself moaning out loud as she lay her legs beside the hair-roughened length of his that she drew blood. Every nerve ending in her body was screaming out in awareness! She tried to blank out the scent and texture of his skin and failed abysmally.

Her damp hair tickled his chin and Quinn's recitation stumbled momentarily as his concentration lapsed. Look on the bright side, mate, he told himself, at least her face is turned away. Schooling his expression into a blank canvas on top of everything else would have been one demand too many.

If he'd needed a reminder that this wasn't about satisfying his frustrated libido, the shocking chill of her slender body through the thin fabric of the top she wore provided it. Several minutes passed—it felt a lot longer to him—and she still didn't relax.

'Comfy?'

Was he joking? 'I'm fine, thank you,' she responded, trying desperately hard not to do anything that might be construed as provocative—she envied Quinn his apparent ability to switch off. 'Not hurting you, am I?'

She tensed all over again as something half between a guttural groan and a gasp escaped his lips. 'What…?' She would have looked to see what was wrong but his open hand moved to the back of her head, holding it where it was on his shoulder.

'Just an elbow in the wrong place,' he explained, adjusting her arm, which was sandwiched between them. 'You feeling any warmer?'

Rowena had been too busy stressing about the physical contact and her lustful thoughts to register that she was feeling less teeth-jarringly icy. 'You know, I think I might be,' she said, her relief showing in her surprised tone.

'I told you so. Now let's speed up the process, shall we?'

Rowena hardly had time to begin wondering in some trepidation what he meant when he began to briskly massage her all over in a detached, businesslike manner. It was obvious the last thing on his mind was sex, which made her feel doubly ashamed of her own fixation.

Even though she had thought it impossible, Rowena did eventually relax, and she even began to enjoy the situation as gradually the hard, tight, circular movements of his hands that had made her skin tingle became long, smooth, sweeping motions that moved from shoulder to flank and back. The combination of the delicious warmth and his clever hands had all the coiled tension in her body seeping slowly away.

She lay there a long time enjoying the physical contact—any contact was better than none, as far as her touch-starved body was concerned—before she finally turned her head to look at him.

His eyes were closed, the shadow of his lashes creating a dark shadow across the jutting line of his cheekbones. Greedily she examined the sharp planes and angular hollows of his face. It wasn't until that moment that she finally accepted just how often during their short period of separation she'd literally ached to look at him.

As if he sensed her scrutiny, Quinn's dark eyelashes began to lift. Rowena froze and she found herself staring into sensational deep aquamarine eyes. Quinn had frustrating eyes that could turn her bones to water and at the same time shield his thoughts totally from her.

Her tentative smile faded as she received none in return. 'I'm *much* warmer.'

'The thaw seems to have gone further than skin-deep.' It was impossible to tell from his dry tone if he thought this was a bad or good thing.

'If you ever want a career change you could make a fortune as a masseur…'

'I'll keep that in mind.'

She hitched herself a little higher so that his fingers, which had been splayed in the small of her back, came to rest on the curve of her firm bottom. She gave a determined little wriggle and sighed. 'That's *so* good, Quinn.'

Quinn's lean fingers spasmed digging into her firm resilient flesh. His hand lifted clear of her skin.

'Sorry.'

His hoarse tone gave her the first hint that he might not be as laid-back about the situation as he'd seemed so far. The discovery made Rowena feel slightly less depraved and more than slightly relieved!

She stretched lazily and gave another sexy, sinuous little wriggle that Quinn had no doubt was *not* accidental, and a pulse beside his mouth began to throb.

Tongue caught between her teeth, she raised herself on one arm and, arching her back, ran a finger casually down his chest. 'My feet are still cold,' she complained, running her toes down his calf to illustrate her claim. 'See…' The borrowed top, which just about skimmed her hips, hiked up as she brought her knee up.

'Shall I warm them on you?' The innocent enquiry was barely out of her mouth when she found herself tipped sideways until they lay shoulder to shoulder.

'Just what the hell do you think you're doing, Rowena?' Smouldering eyes locked with hers.

Her back against the sofa, her front against his front, there wasn't any way Rowena could avoid that accusing glare.

'I don't know what you mean,' she said, not pulling off the dumb act at all convincingly. She sighed as her eyes slid from his. 'I suppose I was being a little...*provocative*...' She was suddenly annoyed with herself for feeling so guilty. Wasn't she a modern woman with needs of her own and as much right as a man to make the first move? She'd read all the articles—hell's bells! She'd written a lot of them.

'Is this Rowena being brutally honest?'

No, this is Rowena saying the first stupid thing that comes into her head! Her antagonism faded perceptibly as she encountered the tender expression in his eyes.

'Is this Quinn rubbing salt in the wound?' She sighed. 'I don't see what's so bad about being provocative...'

'Did I say there was anything wrong?'

'You want an apology? Fine, I'm sorry I came on to you.'

'You're *sorry*,' he parroted hoarsely. The veil of her lashes lifted once more as she heard the rasp of his incredulous inhalation. 'I don't want your apologies, woman, I want *you*!'

Her stomach flipped over. *'You do?'* Her body sagged in relief.

His hand cupped her chin. 'This can't have come as a shock; I've hardly been trying to disguise the fact.'

'Well, no,' she admitted, blushing. 'But that was before you knew…I thought maybe me being pregnant had put you off the…physical side of things, and I'd hate you to think that I was coming on to you because I need a father for the baby,' she rattled on nervously. 'Because *nothing* could be farther from the truth.'

The fingers around her jaw tightened. 'Need has nothing to do with it, Rowena, you've *got* a father for the baby—me!'

'You know what I mean,' she responded, wary of the implacable expression in his eyes.

Oh, he knew what she meant, all right! Perhaps now wasn't the right moment to make it plain to her that he wasn't about to be a part-time father, Quinn thought drily.

'I think I get the general drift…but I'm confused. Why the…*provocation*, after you've been holding me at arm's length?'

Was he joking? There were many men in this world she could safely snuggle with, but Quinn wasn't one of them!

She found she had no control over the direction of her blue eyes as they dropped with embarrassing obviousness from his eyes to his firm, sensual mouth and back again. 'Do we have to analyse this?' she agonised hoarsely, the whole of her restless body burning up with frustrated desire.

'I think maybe we do.' What are you going to do? the voice in his head asked mockingly. Hold out indefinitely? Sure, that's *really* likely!

If this was his way of punishing her, it was working! How could she satisfactorily explain the fact that something just felt *right*. Rowena sighed, and struggled to get her frustration in check. It had reached the point where there seemed little point in prevaricating.

'The thing is, I've been thinking about you…us…well, actually,' she corrected, her lips quivering into a self-derisive curve, 'I've been trying *not* to because—'

'Because your concentration is shot to hell and things like eating are a chore. You laugh at jokes when you haven't heard them and, worst of all…or is it best…?' he recited, his gaze fixed and unblinking, his tone unemotional and flat.

His head went back and Rowena watched completely riveted as the muscles in his strong throat worked.

'The worst thing is when you wake up in the middle of the night, your body aching, and the only person that can take that ache away isn't there.' Lifting a crooked arm to cover his eyes, he suddenly rolled away from her onto his back, his broad, powerful chest heaving.

About mid-way through the final impassioned instalment in his narrative, Rowena had begun to nod wonderingly and she continued to do so even when he stopped speaking.

Ambivalent emotions churned in her stomach. The raw, barely restrained hunger she'd seen in Quinn's face, and discovering they'd been suffering almost identical symptoms, had both frightened and deeply excited her.

'I didn't know you felt like that,' she whispered, raising a hand to the side of his face.

His arm fell away from his eyes. Lips twisted cynically, he scanned her face. 'You didn't want to know.' He caught her wrist and held her fingers there against the day's growth that cast a dark shadow over his lower jaw.

Rowena wasn't prepared to take all the blame. 'I suppose if you hadn't been so stubborn about us having an affair we'd have already got this out of our systems.'

'If it makes you feel better to believe that, Rowena, go right ahead and cling onto that belief.'

'I think maybe the only thing that will make me feel better is feeling you inside me,' she declared boldly. Her eyes glazed hotly as she thought of Quinn's mouth on her skin, his fingers stroking her, Quinn sliding hard into her—and her mouth opened to drag air noisily into her oxygen-depleted lungs.

A groan was ripped from his throat before his mouth came crashing down on hers. Fingers hooked into his hair, Rowena opened her mouth, welcoming the hot, probing invasion of his tongue. Frantically she plastered herself against him, revelling in the pain as the hard swell of his arousal ground into her belly.

'You have no idea,' he rasped, 'how often I've thought about this...'

Rowena nodded, pressing frantic kisses to the curve of his jaw, his throat, his eyelids. 'Oh, but I do,' she cried brokenly. *'I do!'*

His big hands ran down the curve of her spine and, cupping the rounded contours of her bottom, hauled her hard against him. His mouth left hers for a second as he yanked the top over her head. It was closely followed by his own.

His naked flesh touched hers and the fire in her veins exploded, scorching away any residual sanity in its wake. She felt his teeth tug at her lower lip, felt his breath hot and rapid on her cheek as his hands cupped, stroked and squeezed her swollen breasts, catching each engorged pink nipple in turn between his thumb and forefinger and teasing the aching nubs of flesh. Each caress sizzled along her nerve endings, wave after wave of pure sensation that reduced Rowena to a moaning, compliant wreck.

'You like this…?'

Rowena's eyelids felt heavy; it was hard to lift them—but the effort was worth it! God, but he was beautiful!

'I like it.' Her voice sounded as if it were coming from a long way away. Then more firmly, but still trembling and strange, *'A lot!'*

Breathing heavily, she dragged the quilt down to look at all of him—the breath snagged painfully in her throat. He was incredible, she thought, marvelling hungrily at the perfection of his streamlined body. There wasn't an ounce of surplus flesh on his spare frame to hide the stupendous muscular development and the boxers he wore were equally inadequate to hide the extent of his arousal.

'You'll get cold.'

Rowena laughed huskily. That hardly seemed likely; she was burning up, her veins were filled with fire, her throat ached with emotional need. She reached out and touched his flat belly and felt the immediate satisfactory sharp contraction of his strong muscles as he sucked in his breath in a harsh gasp. He let her hands explore some more until they slid a little too low, then, ignoring her protests, caught them in one of his own.

'Too much, too soon,' he explained thickly, pinning both her hands above her head in his capable grasp.

'I can't touch you.'

'But I can touch you.' An insolent, sexual smile curved his lips as she shuddered hard against him. 'You'll like that, won't you…?' His green eyes, smouldering as though they were lit by an inner flame, melded with her own.

'Yes.' She licked her dry lips as her dilated pupils stayed glued to his dark face—she was his utterly, and the unconditional surrender felt strangely liberating. A restless twist of her hips sent the quilt slithering to the floor.

'Don't worry, I'll keep you warm,' he breathed into her mouth.

'Please,' she replied simply.

Quinn looked into her smoky eyes, and what he saw took his breath away.

Rowena shivered, but not from cold this time. Quinn's free hand was on her stomach, and soon his lips were there too, tracing a slow, tingling path across her flesh. She moaned as her insides violently contracted and then did so again and again until she felt she couldn't breathe. Even with her eyes closed the room was spinning.

He pushed her body down under him and loomed over her. This display of masculine strength she would have scorned in her right mind only heightened her escalating, scalding excitement. Watching the play of emotion over her passion-pale features, he slid his hand under the edge of her stretchy smooth pants and felt the betraying heat and slickness between her legs.

The feral sound of her keening wail made him pull back.

Rowena's eyes, the dilated pupils almost obliterating the blue, snapped open. 'Don't stop!' she implored in an agonised whisper. *'Please…!'*

Quinn released her hands and pressed a burning kiss to her parted lips. 'I think you'd be much more comfortable without these…' He fingered the lacy waistband.

'I would—I definitely would.'

What Quinn's actions lacked in finesse as he roughly slid the pants down her long legs he more than made up for in urgency. He parted her legs, need stamped indelibly on his hard-edged features as he savoured the mind-blowingly erotic sight of her sensuous body waiting for him—she was his!

'Now, Quinn, *please*!' Her eyes glowed with a slumberous passion as she parted her legs still wider—it was an invitation that Quinn couldn't and didn't resist.

During the first breathless moment of penetration Rowena, overcome by the sheer blissful wonder of her softness being stretched and filled, just clung, her fingers digging into his back, her long legs wrapped around his waist.

As they moved, hot, slick skin on slick skin, her sense of self disappeared. There was no individual Quinn and Rowena; there was just mindless pleasure and the promise of more held tantalisingly out of reach. Each thrust of his body took her deeper and deeper into the maelstrom of sensation; the blood pounded darkly in her head as his erotic whispers became frantic pants.

She felt the climax coming, building strength inside her before the shattering release actually arrived. Pleasure rolled over her like a tidal wave, bathing each individual cell of her body, stretching each individual sinew and fibre to their limitations. Above her she was conscious of Quinn shuddering and he cried out her name over and over until the final hot, pulsing surges of his body stilled.

Their breathing gradually stilled as they lay tangled together. He would have slid from her then, but Rowena, already half asleep, held him tight.

CHAPTER SIX

ROWENA woke to find herself staring up at a canopy. She blinked as the gold fleur-de-lis embroidered on the deep blue pleated silk slid into focus. She sat up, taking the quilt she was wrapped in with her, and realised she was lying in bed—a very large, carved, dark oak four-poster and one that to her certain knowledge she'd never seen before.

It took her several hazy moments to recall the sequence of events that had taken her to the cottage and this bed. She clutched her tousled blonde head and groaned—talk about complicating things!

Quinn, she reasoned, must have carried her upstairs while she'd slept, slept after…! A tide of heat washed over her body, and hastily she fast-forwarded over what had immediately preceded her falling asleep. It wasn't easy; her thoughts showed a weak tendency to dwell dreamily on her temporary madness.

Gran! Her eyes flew open in alarm and guilt crowded out everything else. While they'd been making love her gran had been fighting for her life. How could I be so shallow…so selfish? she berated herself. Self-disgust churned in her stomach. How long had she slept? It could have been round the clock for all she knew. Her sense of disorientation increased as she looked around wildly for a clock and found none, and the heavy curtains were drawn so it was impossible to gauge the time of day.

Sliding from under the warm covers, Rowena grabbed a light embroidered throw off a small sofa at the foot of the bed to cover her nakedness. Lifting up the tail of the improvised sarong, she then ran over to the window and pushed aside the curtains. She was relieved to see it was still daylight; that relief was tempered by the fact it was still snowing like crazy.

'I thought I heard you moving around.'

Rowena spun to face the figure who had silently materialised in the room, the chinks of light from the disturbed curtains catching her hair, turning it to a bright silver halo around her fine-boned face.

Quinn was no longer in black leather. He now looked equally virile and desirable in a pair of dark moleskin trousers and a chunky knitted cream sweater he'd obviously appropriated.

The owner of the cottage, it would seem, was a big man also. It was hard not to notice that the outfit fitted Quinn's broad-shouldered, long-legged frame extremely well—if a little too snugly in the hip area. Rowena swallowed and brought her restless gaze back to his face.

'You look better,' he announced, after subjecting her pink-cheeked face to a cool-eyed scrutiny. 'Did you sleep well?' he added as his enigmatic eyes continued to scan her wary face as though he expected to see something written on the clear, creamy skin.

Like someone afraid to incriminate herself in an interrogation, Rowena kept her face blank. She nodded awkwardly—after what she'd been imagining his opening comments might be, this innocuous enquiry was actually a relief. She just hoped he kept things simple and didn't start some deeply embarrassing post-mortem, because if he did she didn't know how she was going to explain away her wanton behaviour!

'Too well. What time is it?' she asked, tightening the loop of fabric gathered loosely over her bosom.

Quinn laid down the tray he carried. 'Tea time.' He didn't appear perturbed or particularly surprised by his less than warm reception. 'Will you be mother?' He winced, and straightened up, brushing a stray hank of hair from his eyes. 'Sorry, no pun intended—' he began apologetically.

'For goodness' sake, I'm pregnant—' she responded snappily, ungrateful for his display of consideration. Rowena didn't want consideration, she wanted everything to be the way it had been. *Dream on*, a cruel voice of realism in her head mocked. 'I'm not made of china—don't for heaven's sake start censoring what you say on my account,' she told him in exasperated distaste.

'Right, no special treatment...I'll make a mental note of that,' he promised gravely.

Her eyes narrowed as she tried to detect mockery in his solemn face. 'How long exactly have I been asleep?'

'I don't know *exactly*,' he mocked, mimicking her crisp tone. 'If I'd known it was important I'd have made a note.' Rowena made an impatient sound in the back of her throat. 'It's about four-thirty, if that's any help.'

'Four-thirty—but that's—'

'Halfway between four and five.'

'Half the day's gone!' She gasped, tucking her hair behind her ears in an agitated jerky gesture. 'How could you let me…?' she wailed. She bit her lip and tried to tighten her grip on her self-control and the throw wrapped carelessly around her—an accident waiting to happen. 'I shouldn't be here.' She looked wildly around the room. 'I should be doing…'

'What?' One dark brow quirked and Rowena shook her head, struck dumb by her growing sense of impotence.

Her slender shoulder slumped defeatedly. *'Something,'* she responded in an agonised whisper.

It was hard for Quinn to reconcile the lonely, fragile figure before him with the indelible mental image in his head of that smart-mouthed, feisty lady editor who not only incited respect, lust and insanity in him in about equal measures, but also provided him with a constant, stimulating challenge in a way no other woman had ever done.

He'd always known Rowena had a more vulnerable side; what he hadn't known was how strong his own protective instincts would be on the occasions she revealed it. This wasn't about the fact that she was carrying his child, this was about the fact that he loved her—every time he admitted it to himself it got easier.

One arm extended, he took an impetuous step towards her.

It was too much, too soon for Rowena, who knew that his touch suspended all rational mental processes. She took a stumbling backward step that brought her legs in contact with the low, deep window sill.

There was a self-derisive glitter in Quinn's eyes as his arm fell back to his side. Rowena felt she ought to be pleased by the neutral expression on his normally mobile features when he eventually did speak, but now she found herself wondering about what he was hiding.

'I know you're worried sick about your gran and, left to you, you'd prefer to hike across the Grampians than wait the snow out with me, but the fact is your presence at the hospital is in no way essential to her recovery. She has expert medical care and if she does wake up before you arrive she's surrounded by people who love her…'

'Wake up?' Rowena curtly cut in with a frown.

Quinn sighed, mentally cursing his blunder. 'Just a figure of speech. Do you—?'

She scanned his face. 'She's unconscious, isn't she?' His veiled eyes dropped tellingly and she gasped. 'Why didn't anyone tell me?' Her voice quivered with emotion.

'She had lapsed into coma when I spoke to Niall before we got on the plane,' Quinn admitted quietly. 'He asked me to pass on the information, and I intended to, but you were too upset at the time. I thought I'd wait until later on.'

'Just how much later on did you have in mind?' she asked bitterly as she reviewed all the opportunities he'd had.

'I didn't think telling you would serve any useful purpose. You were already stressed enough and in my judgement you—'

His judgement! Rowena saw red; her bosom swelled wrathfully—the arrogance of the man, the *conceit*! All her life she'd been coming up against exactly this sort of patronising sexual stereotyping, the convenient result of which was that *men* ended up making all the important decisions in life. The way she saw it, masculine concern was very often nothing but another example of male powerplay.

'And *your* judgement is the only one that counts, I take it,' she cut in icily.

Though when he replied Quinn sounded composed, he had no control over the two dark stripes of angry colour that appeared high across his slashing cheekbones. 'I made a call—'

Rowena's hands balled into fists as she impatiently brushed a stray tear from her cheek. 'It wasn't your call to make,' she cut him off furiously.

His big shoulders lifted fractionally. 'And as I was about to say—I'd do the same again,' he announced, condemning himself even further in her eyes by still not displaying any regret whatsoever for the high-handed way he'd acted in withholding the vital piece of information.

'How *dare* you!' She gasped, her blue eyes flashing. 'Ignorance is not bliss, it's just ignorance. The next thing you'll be expecting is my thanks!'

'I didn't do it for your gratitude, Rowena.'

'No, you did it because I'm some pathetic, weak little girlie who needs to be protected from the nasty truth,' she sneered. 'Did it make you feel like the big strong man, keeping me in the dark?' she asked bitterly.

A flicker of something like anger moved at the back of Quinn's eyes. 'I would have told you when I thought the time was right,' he gritted.

That figured. 'When *you* thought…oh, that's all right, then,' she trilled nastily.

'You want the truth, Rowena, great, that's absolutely fine by me.' With her back already literally against the wall, this time there was nowhere for her to retreat when he advanced menacingly towards her. 'For instance, we could stop pretending we both don't know the real reason you're prepared to behave with all the native nous of a lemming to get to your grandmother is because you're torn apart with guilt. Tell me, how many invitations have you refused during the past twelve months?' he continued inexorably when she shook her head in mute, horrified denial.

The last remaining shreds of colour faded from Rowena's cheeks.

'You're eaten up with remorse every time you think about all the time you *didn't* spend with her because your high-powered career was so much more important than visiting with elderly relatives.'

He must think I'm a total bitch, she thought, steeling herself to meet his angrily scornful eyes squarely just as the heat appeared to be fading from them. Considering the fact that she had always known Quinn had a capacity for displaying great ruthlessness when he wanted to, she ought to have known better than to actually request him not to treat her with kid gloves. Quinn also had a capacity for tenderness and compassion, which in her self-righteous indignation she'd condemned him for—it wasn't really surprising he'd hit back.

'I think you've made your point, Quinn,' she murmured unhappily.

Quinn had been feeling lousy even before her dignified response. He deeply regretted allowing her to goad him into making such brutal remarks.

'That was unjustified. I'm—'

'No, it's true, I'm selfish and self-centred—'

Quinn shook his head.

'Not to mention very close to feeling sorry for myself,' she added with a small, forced laugh.

'When you're focused on one thing it's easy to lose sight of the big picture,' he told her, laying a tentative hand on her shoulder, his fingers tightening slightly when she didn't immediately reject his touch. 'As for people around us, we all of us take them for granted. Why, I've lost count of the number of girlfriends who have accused me of always putting them second to my job.'

Rowena wondered wryly whether this timely reminder of his diverse and extensive selection of sexual partners was meant to cheer her up—if so it was a major miscalculation! She had difficulty controlling the nauseous feelings of jealousy his *soothing* words evoked.

Quinn lifted a strand of lint-fair hair in his fingers and let it fall again. He tucked her chin into the angle of his jaw and hugged her. 'Loss of consciousness in your grandmother's condition is not unusual and it doesn't mean she couldn't eventually make a full recovery.'

Hands on his forearms, Rowena pulled away from the light embrace. 'You're not just saying that?' she pleaded, not daring to allow herself to read too much into his words.

He caught her chin in his hand and smiled ruefully down into her upturned features. 'What, and treat you like someone who can't take it on the chin? I wouldn't dare!' His expression grew sober. 'Seriously, Rowena, I don't want to raise any false hopes, but there's no point assuming the worst. In fact, instead of stressing, I think we should be thanking our lucky stars. It could have been a lot worse.'

Rowena gaped incredulously up at him. His tall, dynamic figure made a most unlikely Pollyanna. 'How, exactly?'

The curtains rings rattled as he reached over her shoulder and pulled them apart.

Taking her by the shoulders, he turned her bodily around one hundred and eighty degrees. 'We could be out there,' he said, nodding pointedly at the frosty wilderness outside. Rowena shuddered and leant back and retreated into the warm solidity of his chest. 'So I suggest we make the best of the situation. It's not perfect, but—'

'You don't say!' Despite everything, his painfully upbeat attitude was amusing.

'For one thing the décor up here is a bit too…' head on one side, she watched him consider the ornate furnishings and bold colour scheme in the large room '…*gothic* for my taste, but you'll be pleased to hear that the monster stove below has hotplates and can not only boil a kettle, it also heats the water—you know what that means.'

'I do?'

'Baths,' he declared with lip-smacking relish. 'And I have nothing but admiration for the bathing facilities. You could fit an army in the tub—go take a look,' he advised, steering her in the right direction. 'On second thoughts, try the tea first—brewed with my own fair hands. There was only dried milk, but it's drinkable.'

Now that he mentioned it, tea did sound rather good. She touched the tip of her tongue to her dry lips and approached the tea-tray perched a bit precariously on the side of the bed. As she sat down she was careful not to dislodge it.

'Are you hungry?' he asked, watching with amusement as she sipped the hot drink, an expression of blissful concentration on her face. 'Because there's not a bad selection of dried goods on offer and, as the deep freeze is beginning to defrost without power, I think we're almost morally obliged to eat some of the stuff before it wastes.'

Rowena had some problems with his logic, but she was hungry and she admitted as much.

'And then there's the clothes problem…not that I have any problem with your present outfit.'

His slow, sensual smile made her heart race painfully. 'I did notice that you've solved your own clothes problem,' she retorted, her own glance moving hurriedly from his thigh area where her errant gaze showed a marked tendency to linger.

Quinn pushed the ribbed cuffs of the sweater he wore up over the tanned skin of his forearms. 'Not too bad, is it? he mused complacently.

Rowena tore her flustered gaze from the hair-roughened skin he'd revealed. 'And they call women the vain ones!' she retorted hoarsely.

With a grin Quinn strutted towards her and struck a dramatic pose in front of one of the large ornate mirrors that filled the room. They were so numerous that it meant it was hard to stand anywhere in the room and not see yourself. Personally Rowena found it disturbing to repeatedly catch glimpses of someone who looked like her, but was in some obscure way different—something about the eyes…?

'When I think that I blew my one big chance at a modelling career…' he bemoaned, throwing her a look of mock dejection.

'"Mirror, mirror on the wall, who's the fairest…?"' Her teasing grin faded as it dawned on her that the answer to that question for her at least would always be Quinn. 'You didn't say—did you see anything I could wear?'

'No, this is definitely a male domain, nothing in the cupboards screams female—well, that's not strictly true,' he conceded. 'I did find several odd items, all assorted sizes, if you get my drift...'

Rowena looked puzzled. 'I don't.'

Quinn's expression of frank disbelief faded to amusement as it dawned on him she was actually being serious—for a woman who had written some very cynical articles in her time about male infidelity, Rowena had a charmingly innocent streak.

'Put it this way, I don't think our absentee host is heavily into monogamy.'

Perhaps this blushing thing was physiological—something to do with her pregnancy. She hoped it was only a temporary aberration because it definitely wasn't in keeping with her hard-nosed image at all.

'In fact, a man after your own heart,' she commented lightly.

The smile in Quinn's eyes sparkled some more in a frighteningly charismatic way. 'Now that I come to think about it, there was this very nice basque in a thirty-six D...I don't suppose you could find some use for it...?' he wondered innocently.

Rowena's teeth came together in a ferocious fake smile. 'The only use I'd have for a D cup is to hold my laundry!' she declared with a wistful peek down at her chest.

Quinn threw back his head and his big booming laughter rang out. It was as warm and uninhibited as the man himself, she found herself thinking as he wiped tears of mirth from his face.

'It's extremely insensitive—not to mention callous—to treat a woman's physical shortcomings as a joke,' she informed him tartly.

The attractive laughter lines around his eyes smoothed out as their glances collided. 'You don't have any physical shortcomings,' he announced abruptly. His eyes continued to devour her hungrily for several paralysing seconds before he got to his feet. 'You have a good rummage for something to wear and I'll sort out some food.'

Rowena, who found she had been holding her breath during that prolonged eye contact, released a long, shuddering sigh when she was left alone.

Maybe, she pondered as she carefully sorted through the drawers of neatly folded clothes, it was a mistake to act as if the air didn't crackle with electricity when they were in a room together. It wasn't unreasonable to suppose that he'd want to do something about that sizzle once their more urgent needs like shelter and food were dealt with. Quinn's old hunter-gatherer instinct had obviously kicked in strongly—especially after she'd all but ravished him earlier! You couldn't just blow hot and cold on the man without offering some sort of explanation, no matter how lame.

Perhaps she should tackle the problem head on and tell him—Sleeping together means nothing, Quinn, she could say. Sex is no basis for a long-term relationship, and even if I were into long-term relationships…which I'm not…I can't risk falling in love. It's a genetic thing; all the women in my family go a little strange when they fall in love.

No, if she told him that he'd just think she was crazy.

After due consideration what she actually said when she emerged downstairs was, 'That smells nice.'

She noticed her favourite Gucci boots, barely recognisable in the their scuffed, battered condition, sitting forlornly beside the hot stove. She accepted their demise more philosophically than she would have a few hours earlier, when things like what she was wearing had still seemed important.

Perhaps near-death experiences did that to a person…?

Not that she could claim to be *totally* unconcerned about her appearance. Quinn, with his unstudied elegance, was the sort of man who made women conscious of their appearance. As she recalled the advice of a lady who had once been a top model Rowena's head went up and her shoulders back as she crossed the room towards him. 'It's not what you wear, darling,' she'd told Rowena, 'it's the way you wear it. If you carry yourself well you can look stylish in a sack.' Well, what she was wearing now had to be one up from a sack!

'Mushroom risotto, made with some dried shitake and chanterelles. Pass that saffron, would you…?' Quinn requested without removing his gaze from the large open pan he was stirring.

Rowena who had spent a long time fussing stupidly over her appearance—which, when your dress was a man's baggy jumper and your footwear was wrinkled woolly socks, was pretty sad—experienced a totally irrational feeling of pique as she did as he requested.

'This is definitely what I'd term back to basics,' she observed, getting a closer look on the large pan perched on the cast-iron hotplate atop the room heater. Her forearm accidentally nudged his as she handed him the spice.

'Sorry.'

Quinn turned his hand over, but instead of closing his long fingers around the spice pot he looked back and forth from the sleeve of his jumper to the almost identical sleeves of the one she wore. A slow grin spread across his ruggedly handsome face; the comparison seemed to amuse him. He lightly touched the fine-boned delicacy of her blue-veined wrist, feeling the echo of a strong pulse as his finger skated along the bony projection beneath her thumb. Again the contrast fascinated him, but not in a way this time that brought a smile to his lips.

His eyes lifted and skimmed her face, taking in the big, dilated pupils and the half-scared, half-defiant expression on her delicately flushed English-rose face. Rowena was perfectly still, her eyes focused on his mouth, and each breath she took was an effort.

Abruptly he dropped her wrist and, taking the spice pot from her lax grip, turned back to the cooking pot, leaving her to wonder whether what had happened had been a figment of her imagination.

'We could buy matching anoraks too.'

Suffering from the effects of severe anticlimax, Rowena lowered her eyes and tried to distance herself from the ache deep inside. 'If I was ever seen in an anorak my career would be in tatters.'

'You used to say that about having a baby,' he reminded her, sprinkling some of the fragrant golden saffron threads into the cooking mixture.

Rowena watched the saffron melt into the creamy dish, her whole body rigid with tension. 'So I did.'

Quinn tasted a spoonful of creamy rice mixture and gave a satisfied grunt. 'Don't look so worried. Given your well-known views on the subject of executives with babies, I expect there'll be a few sly nudges at first, but we can weather it,' he announced confidently, placing the cooking pot on the table. 'Could you pass down a couple of plates...?' He nodded towards the shelf behind her.

His benevolent line in advice set Rowena's teeth on edge. Mouth set in a hard line, she reached up and did as he requested, blissfully unaware that the sweater she wore as a dress rode indecently high over her smooth hips as she did so. But Quinn noticed.

She brought the plates crashing down on the wooden surface beside the steaming pot. She glared at him and he looked back, looking distinctly shifty.

'What's wrong?' he asked warily.

Rowena folded her arms across her chest. 'Where do I start?' The streaks of heat across his cheekbones, no doubt as a result of his time spent huddled over the hot stove, seemed to be fading. 'Firstly, there is no *we*.'

Quinn smiled thinly as he surveyed her flushed, antagonistic face. 'It's good to see a bit of colour back in your cheeks. And second? I take it there is a second...?' he speculated drily.

'*Second*,' she bit back obligingly, 'I haven't changed my mind about anything at all. I still think that you can't be a good wife and mother and have enough left for your career.'

Quinn's expression hardened, and eyes as merciless as the sea swept her face. 'Then you didn't mean it when you said that you were keeping...?'

'I did mean it,' she retorted impatiently. 'I am going to keep the baby.' She saw a wave of palpable relief pass over his tense features and tried not to soften her resolve.

There were big changes ahead for her and she was scared. She couldn't admit this to Quinn, but she could make him appreciate that insulting her intelligence by acting as if there would be no problem was not on!

His eyes narrowed cynically. 'Do I hear a *but* coming on…?'

'*But* I'm trying to be realistic. There aren't enough hours in the day to do my job as well as I'd like to now.'

'You could always move into the office, or maybe not sleep at all.'

'I can do without the constant stream of facetious interruptions!'

'Consider my lips sealed,' he returned with mock humility.

Rowena thought it best not to consider his lips at all but, despite her caution, her stomach muscles tightened. 'If there aren't enough hours in the day now…when a demanding baby comes along…' She gave an eloquent shrug.

'You want a pat on the back for your noble sacrifice—fine, but while you're being *realistic*, Rowena, it might be a good idea to remember that babies don't just demand, they give too…'

Rowena stiffened at the reprimand in his voice. Resentment swelled in her tight chest. Sure, Quinn could afford to sneer at realism while she was doing the worrying for both of them.

All he'd have to do was buy a new wallet to accommodate a few snapshots of his new baby and make the odd weekend free for a walk in the park. The fact that she'd have treated any suggestion that he might be anything more than a token presence in the baby's life with extreme hostility didn't affect her seething resentment.

'I'm aware of that.' She sniffed coldly. 'Deciding to keep the baby wasn't a sentimental decision…' Sentimentality implied something superficial, and something far deeper and more profound, something she still didn't understand herself, had motivated Rowena when she'd decided she wanted to keep this baby.

'No, I can see that sentimentality would not be in keeping with your image.'

Her fingernails inscribed deep half-moons in the soft flesh of her palms as her hands balled into tight fists. He seemed determined to misinterpret everything she said.

'I don't have an image!'

Her teeth grated as one dark, eloquent brow lifted in silent scepticism.

'What, not even the *ice-maiden*?' he wondered, affecting surprise. His expression hardened. 'Come off it, Rowena! People think you recharge your batteries at night, not sleep, and you play up to the role for all it's worth. I'm not saying there's a problem with that if it works for you; the problem arises when you carry on playing the role at home. *Home*, the place where you chill out, have a few beers with friends—cast your memory back, Rowena, you're sure to remember what it's like.' His lip curled as his scornful gaze travelled over her body. 'Or maybe not?'

He silently despaired at the fact that even in the midst of the heated row the promise of slim curves beneath the shapeless covering had an instant effect on his libido. He could almost feel the soft peach down of her skin. He shifted his stance uncomfortably—it was a strong effect, and not the sort that was easy to hide. It was the sort of effect that told Rowena it didn't matter if she acted like a total bitch—Quinn Tyler was still a complete pushover when it came to her!

He needn't have worried because Rowena's eyes didn't leave his contemptuous face.

For the sort of lifestyle Quinn described, you needed friends, Rowena thought dully. Over the years her circle had not expanded, but got smaller.

At least she now knew what Quinn really thought about her. Given his strongly expressed views it seemed pretty obvious that it wasn't pleasure in her company that made him seek her out—that left her body and sex.

It wasn't the first time a man had wanted her for her body—it was the first time the knowledge had hurt and depressed her this much!

Well, it was good that was sorted, she told herself bracingly. At least she wouldn't embarrass them both by reading anything deep and meaningful into his pursuit.

'I suppose that makes me the person you'd least like to be stuck in a blizzard with. Bad luck, Quinn, but I suppose those are the breaks…'

She exhaled through her quivering nostrils. It didn't seem likely that Quinn would believe what she was about to say, but she knew it was important for her to try—for some reason, Quinn's opinion mattered to her.

'Don't laugh.' This didn't look likely. 'But if you must know, I'm keeping the baby because I've discovered I'm as genetically programmed to protect this new life as the next woman…' A knot of emotion ached in her throat as she met his eyes—he was still displaying no inclination to laugh, but she thought she did see something close to shock move at the back of his eyes. 'It came as just as much of a shock to me.' Her quick, self-derisive smile held no humour.

It had been more than a simple shock; for someone who had been fighting against genetic programming most of her life, this was an incredibly hard admission to make to herself, let alone a second party—especially a second party who was personally involved.

'I'm not shocked, Rowena,' he replied, his voice surprisingly gentle. 'I'm sure you'll make a great mother.'

'I'm glad one of us is.' His gentleness was nearly her undoing. She felt the tears sting her eyelids as she blinked rapidly, her eyes focusing on the steaming plate of food he slid in front of her.

'I've never had a broody moment in my life.' A baby deserves a better mother than me, she decided as a fresh batch of doubts assailed her.

'You've never been pregnant before either. At least I'm assuming…?'

Rowena was amazed to see her fingers curled against the darker skin of his wrist. Her sensitive stomach flipped over before she self-consciously released him and picked up a fork.

'No, I've never been pregnant before,' she enunciated in a clear, icy voice. 'Have you?' She was already deeply regretting going public with her interlude of self-doubt.

Quinn was undoubtedly ruthless and sneaky enough to turn any weakness she displayed to his own advantage. The problem was, she didn't yet know what he did want.

Quinn grinned and began to rub his wrists. 'No, I've no experience to speak of, but I expect we'll muddle through somehow…'

That *we* word again! And she didn't know how anyone could look cheerful at the prospect of *muddling* through! Muddling through filled her with deep horror. Right now her head was filled with so much muddle, half the time she didn't know her own name. Why, she was so muddled that, until he'd revealed exactly what he thought about her, she'd even questioned if it were possible Quinn hadn't fallen in love with her—you couldn't get more muddled than that!

'Is there something wrong with your short-term memory, Quinn? I've already told you there is no *we*! There is not going to be any cosy scene of domestic bliss. I may be pregnant but some things haven't changed. I don't require a husband.'

'I don't recall asking you to marry me.'

Rowena experienced an unexpected and totally perverse pang of abandonment. 'Good, that saves me the embarrassment of refusing you. This is very good,' she added brightly as she placed a forkful of risotto into her mouth.

'And as always your concern for my feelings is uppermost.'

This time there was no mistaking his sarcasm. Rowena chewed nervously on her full lower lip.

'I'm sorry if I hurt you, Quinn.' If he hadn't been so stubborn they could have had a nice time with no complications—at least, they could have if she hadn't got pregnant. 'But I told you my terms in New York—'

'Terms!' he exploded, his face darkening with anger. 'Good God, woman this isn't a business negotiation we're discussing, it's a love affair.'

'I would never have a love affair with someone who yells at me!' She shied away as he put out a hand towards her. A frustrated sound escaped from between Quinn's bared teeth as his hand came down with a bang on the table surface.

'I think I've some excuse for yelling. Why didn't you tell me about the baby, Rowena?'

Rowena looked into his dark, impossibly attractive face and accepted what she'd been fighting against: she was in love with Quinn Tyler, and no matter how many telephone numbers she changed or how many miles she put between them, nothing was going to change that!

The world spun and Rowena thought she might faint. She had put her faith in the theory that if a person took sensible precautions she could avoid falling in love. Discovering that her theory was seriously flawed left Rowena with no place to hide.

Rowena hadn't had to look very far to see how love could dramatically change women. Loving Grandpa had made Gran abandon a glittering career without a second thought, and it hadn't stopped there—oh, no! After she'd married Dad her mother had rejected the exciting uncertainty of life as a budding young actress in favour of the security of life as a drama teacher, trying to teach a bunch of unappreciative kids who'd have preferred to be watching cartoons to the delights of Shakespeare. Now all she had was a scrapbook collection of yellowing newspaper reviews which Rowena had once found her weeping over. And now sensible Holly was jumping headlong into marriage with Niall, despite his dismal track record and the fact they had nothing whatever in common and at a point when distractions could be fatal to her fantastic career prospects!

At least *they* had all had the comfort of knowing the men they loved were equally as soft in the head when it came to them. I've gone one better, I've fallen in love with a man who has never used the 'L' word, not even once! Rowena thought frantically.

'Slow down, Rowena, you're hyperventilating… *Rowena*!' Quinn repeated sharply.

He touched her shoulder and she pulled back, her eyes wide and hostile. 'I'm fine…' Slowly her breathing slowed and the red dots dancing before her eyes retreated. 'I wasn't ready to tell you. I didn't even know at that stage what my plans were.'

'And now you do?'

'I'll hand in my notice, of course.' She was winging it and trying simultaneously to give the impression she'd given the whole thing a lot of intelligent thought—she could hardly say she was having trouble thinking a minute ahead. 'Freelance writing is an option, I do have excellent contacts.'

'Hand in your notice! Are you insane?'

This scathing judgement seemed bang on to Rowena, who was wondering what she thought she was doing, blurting out the first rash thing that had come into her head. Only stubborn pride stopped her admitting she'd just been sounding off, that she actually didn't know what she was going to do.

A look of tired comprehension spread across Quinn's strained face as their eyes met. 'Oh, I get it, this is a matter of principle, I suppose…' He was finding it increasingly difficult to abide by his earlier resolve not to get too confrontational or heavy while Rowena was very obviously still pretty traumatised by their snowy adventure.

Rowena was perturbed to discover Quinn didn't appear too impressed by her sacrifice—actually he looked blazing mad.

'Principle *and* practicality, but, yes, it would be hypocritical to do anything else.'

Why didn't she just say, You've ruined my life, Quinn, and have done with it? He thought. 'And you're never hypocritical, I suppose. My God!' he exclaimed bitterly, raking a hand roughly through his dark hair. There was a limit to how much rubbish a man could listen to! 'Do you know, at times you can be the most stiff-necked and pompous woman I've ever met! You're totally obsessed with image. Do you ever consider anyone else but yourself and what *you* want?'

Rowena flinched at the ferocity of this unexpected tirade. Somewhere an image of Gran appeared, her robust frame frail, the intelligent light in her eyes dimmed… 'That's not true!' she gasped weakly.

Quinn's lips twisted in a sardonic smile that left his marvellous eyes cold and hostile. Rowena found it hard to recognise this Quinn in the laconic, laid-back individual she knew.

'*Really?* I must have missed you asking me how *I* feel about becoming a father.' He saw the flare of startled dismay in her eyes and refused to let it soften his resolve. He'd respected her hormones, repressed his baser instincts until she'd asked him not to, and given the best interpretation he knew how of an enlightened, modern man who respected a woman's wishes, but there came a point when enough was enough and he'd passed it! 'Have you even *thought* about it?'

Rowena felt her face colour guiltily. 'I've already told you...' she faltered uncertainly '...I thought I ought to sort out how I felt first.'

'I thought you had it all sorted, down to the big grand gesture of quitting your job,' he mocked. 'And don't try telling me that's got anything to do with not being able to combine motherhood and a career.' He shook his head. 'Sure, you'd take a bit of stick, but with a bit of humour you'd weather it. Oh, sorry,' he drawled, 'I was forgetting you never learnt how to laugh at yourself. Hell, talk about going from the sublime to the ridiculous! You'll pack in the job you've always wanted just because—'

His reaction struck her as the height of perversity. Since when had Quinn rated what she did? 'Who said I always wanted it?' she snarled back.

'You did, and even if you hadn't I think I'd have guessed, seeing as how you went for it like a heat-seeking missile, and displayed just about as much consideration for anything and anybody that got in your way.'

So not only did he think she was a work-obsessed automaton, he thought she was a ruthless operator who wouldn't know an ethic if it poked her in the nose!

Rowena turned away and didn't see the expression of consternation that flickered across his face. When she turned back her chin was up and her eyes were glistening defiantly.

'I'm sorry if my methods offend your fine sensibilities.'

Quinn grimaced and wondered if he was going to stop saying the wrong thing any time soon. 'Rowena…'

Shaking her head, she stepped back before his fingers could grip her shoulder. 'I suppose,' she mused with a small, bitter smile, 'that I should be grateful you didn't accuse me of sleeping my way to the top!' With a sharp, angry twist of her head she sent a heavy strand of hair that lay across her cheek whipping backwards.

'*Hardly*—you've not allowed any precious time in your schedule for anything as frivolous as a love life.'

Rowena didn't bother denying this disdainful observation—partly because there was a lot of truth in it. 'I suppose you'd think better of me if I'd slept with anything with a pulse, like you! Oh, *no*,' she sneered, not allowing him an opportunity to respond. 'Then I'd have been a tart.' Her eyes blazed as she dwelt on the unfairness of it. 'And don't give me any of your ''this is the twenty-first century'' enlightened stuff; men like you, no matter what they say, always have double standards.'

Quinn stood there watching her bosom heave in agitation. 'How many lovers have you actually had?'

The outrageous question coming totally out of the blue disconcerted Rowena almost as much as the gleam in his half-closed eyes.

'I...what...? None of your business!' Outrage brought a rush of fresh colour to her pale cheeks and stiffened her spine to ramrod rigidity.

Quinn was unrepentant. 'Five, twenty...' One dark brow lifted. 'More...*less*?'

'Why do you want to know? Other than nasty, prurient curiosity, that is,' she said, her lips quivering in distaste.

'Well, you weren't on the pill...and you weren't carrying any condoms...' Not the normal behaviour of a sexually active woman, in his experience.

'Which hardly makes me a virgin.' Just a reckless fool with no self-control where Quinn Tyler was concerned.

'No, just not the person best qualified to write some of the articles you have been responsible for.'

'Which you've read, I suppose?' she drawled sarcastically.

'I've seen enough to recognise a common theme.'

'Prove it,' she challenged, calling his bluff. She was pretty sure he had never read a word she'd written.

'Let me see…' Rowena's smug smile broadened as he appeared to flounder. '"Men have been doing it for years, now it's our turn"…?' She was no longer smiling. '"Cheat, but don't get caught." Would you say that's a fair selection of your more grabbable titles?'

'You're taking it totally out of context!' she accused hotly. 'I never advocated casual sex. In fact, I've frequently pointed out that many woman feel pressurised by the media to act like some sort of sex addicts when a great many of us would actually prefer a good book and a box of chocolates,' she explained, with a pitying sniff of feminine disdain.

'That surely would depend on what sort of lover they had.' A dangerous grin slashed his lean features as his lashes lifted to reveal an equally menacing glitter in his eyes.

The prickle under Rowena's skin—a constant companion when Quinn was around—became a raw pain as she was hit by a wave of sexual longing so strong that for several moments her vocal cords were literally paralysed.

'And I suppose if it was Quinn Tyler she'd not want to get out of bed all weekend...?' she finally managed to retort huskily. The second the words were out of her mouth the images started playing in her head of the varied methods Quinn could and in all probability *had* used to keep his partners too exhausted to get out of bed.

'I hate to sound conceited, but that's not a situation without precedent.' He smiled wolfishly.

Before she'd been on the receiving end of that smile Rowena had fondly imagined 'weak-kneed' was just a figure of speech—now she knew differently.

She took a deep gulp and plunged on defiantly, trying to focus on anything but his eyes. 'And recently I've been researching an interesting article on celibate marriages...'

'Celibate marriages?' he repeated incredulously. 'Whatever will they think of next?' he hooted.

Rowena listened to his predictable male reaction with a pitying smile. 'There's nothing new about celibate marriages. Actually there are a lot of people out there who lead a perfectly fulfilling life without sex—*out of choice*—and before you start I have to tell you I've heard every crass joke about Viagra there is. Why assume a sexless marriage is a loveless marriage? I expect reactions like yours are why people aren't inclined to go public about it. Not that I'd expect *you* to appreciate the relief some people experience when you take all the—'

'Passion and excitement?'

His flip interruption earned him a stern frown—the sort that made cocky assistant editors feel insecure. Unfortunately it didn't have a similar dampening effect on Quinn.

'Passion and excitement rarely make it past the first year…'

'That's longer than your boyfriends, so I hear tell,' he responded promptly.

Rowena kept a hold on her temper with difficulty. 'Platonic love has more staying power,' she gritted. 'And some people prefer the less volatile emotions like companionship and affection. Mutual respect,' she added, dogged determination creeping into her tone as she refused to be influenced by his amused scepticism.

She might even appreciate the irony one day in singing the praises of celibacy when her brain was filled to the brim with steamy sexy images—but not in the foreseeable future, she decided as a ribbon of cold sweat slid down her spine!

'Is there some reason you can't have mutual respect and passion?'

'Men,' she retorted, 'are notoriously incapable of juggling more than one task. I think the same goes for emotions. They respect their mothers, they love their children and they lust after their nubile secretaries,' announced the woman who despised generalisations. The same woman who had an article on her laptop detailing the unfair press men received in the media these days. She wondered what Quinn would make of, 'Has the balance swung too far in the other direction?' She'd regretfully decided, 'Are we castrating our men?' might be a bit too strong for the magazine's target audience.

'My secretary is called Vincent and at a guess I'd say the idea of me being consumed by lust would alarm him deeply…'

'You know what I mean,' she snapped crossly.

He nodded. 'Sure, men are shallow, sex-crazed monsters about covers it, I think. Well, as fascinating as the subject of other people's sex lives—or, in this case, *lack* of them—is, we're rather slipping from the point here.'

Just as well he'd remembered his point, because all she could concentrate on now was the flickering images in her head and what upped the agony factor was the fact that Quinn's eager victim was no longer anonymous. She saw that same face every time she looked in the mirror.

'You're usually such a cautious person.' His puzzled eyes moved over her face, noting several signs of strain there, including pinpricks of moisture beading her upper lip which he immediately fantasised about blotting with his own tongue before he— Don't go there, Quinn, he instructed himself urgently. *Too late!*

'I'm sure you've never left your car door unlocked in your life, and I'd have sworn that you've never left home without a tissue or other female essentials…'

And obviously the women Quinn knew thought of condoms as essentials. Come to think of it, a rival magazine that had done a piece on the average contents of the handbag of a woman between the ages of twenty-five and thirty had thought so too, so possibly it was she who was wildly out of step with the times.

'Is that meant to be a crude analogy? Because if so—'

'Hold up,' he protested, holding up a hand to defend his innocence. 'No analogy, crude or otherwise, no *double* or single *entendre*, even. I was just making an observation that you're a very careful person—and before you jump down my throat again I'm not saying that's a bad thing, I'm just pointing out it was a bit out of character.'

'It was a bit out of character for me to sleep with you…'

'It was, but now I'm happy to say it's becoming a regular occurrence.'

Rowena closed her eyes—she'd walked right into that one! She tried not to let her thoughts get sidetracked. It was not easy, but she needed all her wits about her if she wasn't going to reveal something that would only make it harder to say no when Quinn made his next move. It didn't seem overly conceited to think he would at some point—if he hadn't throttled her in the meantime. It was hard to remember, with all this aggression floating around, that they'd once had such an easy rapport.

A nasty thought occurred to her. 'I hope you're not trying to imply it's *my* fault I'm pregnant?' she began. 'Is that where this is leading? Because if you are—'

'It's no more your fault than it is mine.'

Which, Rowena recognised immediately, wasn't the same thing as saying either of them was innocent.

'The only blameless person here is the baby.' His long-lashed eyes dropped to Rowena's flat belly. 'I don't think there's much to be gained from apportioning blame…God!' He groaned, immediately contradicting himself. 'It's no excuse, I know, but I've never had a condom tear on me before…'

The colour faded from her cheeks. 'A condom tore? So that's how…I did wonder, because you were so careful…' Well, that was one mystery solved, but it opened up another. 'And you knew? Why didn't you *say* something?'

'I did, you said it didn't matter. *Actually*,' he recalled, a contemplative gleam in his eyes, 'you said nothing mattered except—'

'Yes, well, there's no point in post-mortem,' Rowena cut in brightly—reminders of what she'd said she could do without.

Actually Quinn had turned out to be very responsive to requests and even orders in her more urgent moments. It had never occurred to Rowena before that you could actually lead a man where you wanted him to go, and Quinn had displayed an amazing talent for interpreting her most inarticulate pleas.

'I suppose you realise it's the height of bad manners to quiz a woman on her sexual history,' she added darkly. 'If you must know, I've had enough lovers.'

'And were any of these numerous relationships long-lived?'

'I didn't say there were *lots*, just enough, and I've never had any interest in long-term relationships…' she countered evasively.

'How could I have forgotten?' he drawled at his driest. 'I hate to ruin all your plans to be a struggling single parent who's *nobly* sacrificed her career for her baby…' Rowena got the distinct impression he wasn't sold on nobility '…but,' he continued, his voice grim, his expression uncompromising, 'this baby has *two* parents, and most people would expect a man in my position to give financial support. In fact,' he added, 'some people might expect me to do more…more as in marry you,' he added when her blank expression of wary incomprehension didn't lift.

Very aware of his keen eyes on her face, Rowena kept her expression very still. 'Well, luckily for you I'm not one of them.' She even managed a passable laugh.

'I'll take that as a no, shall I…?'

Rowena frowned. He didn't sound like a man who'd just had a lucky escape.

'Well, if you don't want to marry me, perhaps it would be better all round if I took responsibility for the baby after the birth. Personally I don't think it can be good for a kid's emotional development to have a mother who never stops reminding him or her of how great a career she could have had if she hadn't sacrificed her all on the altar of maternal love. No,' he mused, his eyes as hard as flint as they surveyed her face. 'The more I think about it, the more sensible it seems. That way your meteoric rise need not be disrupted… If you carry on the way you are, in another couple of years you'll never write another word—but, my, you'll be powerful and that's what counts, isn't it?'

Leaving her sitting there with her mouth open, her face white with stunned disbelief, Quinn casually picked up his plate and left the table.

CHAPTER SEVEN

FOR several seconds Rowena sat there too shocked to respond. She had wondered what Quinn wanted from her, now she knew—he wanted her baby!

Not only did he want the baby, it was equally obvious he didn't really want her—not even as an optional extra! You couldn't class his brief reference to marriage as a real proposal! No, all Quinn wanted was a walking incubator, she thought as a blinding wave of rage washed over her.

With a wrathful cry she suddenly leapt to her feet, slithering a little on the smooth stone floor in her stockinged feet. She righted herself and, with her hands planted firmly on her sashaying hips, advanced threateningly towards the tall figure who was stacking dirty dishes as if he'd not just as good as tried to kidnap her unborn child.

Rowena waited for a few impatient toe-tapping seconds for him to acknowledge her presence before she lost patience—she was in no mood to be ignored—and prodded him in the back.

'You'll have this baby over my dead body!' With an exclamation of frustration she ripped away the tea towel he'd been drying his hands on. 'For heaven's sake you're not in Theatre and washing up isn't a sterile procedure!' she hissed.

'Force of habit.'

'Is that all you've got to say?'

One corner of Quinn's mouth lifted in a contemptuous curl as he surveyed her animated and angry features with cold, unfriendly eyes. 'What do you want me to say?'

'A grovelling apology would be a good start.'

'I'd have thought you'd have welcomed the idea,' he riposted languidly. 'I mean, you obviously think our child is nothing more than an inconvenience.'

'How *dare* you look down your superior nose at me?' she exploded, her hands balling into tight fists of frustration. 'At least I've not bought into the glossy magazine image of a glowing mother and shiny new baby.'

'So now you're the expert? Been moonlighting for one of those pregnancy magazines? Or has your magazine done a spread on designer outfits for the well-dressed newborn?' His scorn brought an angry flush to her cheeks.

'You're a patronising pig!' she told him with complete conviction.

'Maybe I am, but it still doesn't alter the fact that I've encountered a few more mothers and babies in my time than you,' he retorted drily, recalling his exhausting stint on Obs and Gynae when newly qualified. 'I've actually delivered my share of healthy babies.' He didn't add that he wouldn't care to be put in a position where he had to do so again.

'It's what happens when they leave the hospital I'm thinking about.' She didn't dare think about what went before, after the one glimpse she'd taken inside the medical textbook Holly had left at her place. The peek had left her glassy-eyed and panic-stricken. 'Let me tell you about motherhood. I've seen friends, who thought nothing of clubbing it to dawn the night before an important breakfast meeting, crawl into work after having a baby with bags under their eyes beyond even your capability of fixing. They are barely able to keep their eyes open past ten a.m. and ring the nanny with anxiety attacks at least ten times a morning. As for the glossy pictures…' she snorted derisively '…I've been around when they take those. For every one that's printed there are fifty where the baby is throwing up or screaming inconsolably.'

Breathless, she prodded him once more, this time in the chest. It was no more yielding than his stony, uninterested expression.

'And what makes you think you could be a better parent than me?' she demanded. 'Just because you can knock up a meal out of a store cupboard.' She gestured to the neglected risotto sitting sadly on her plate. 'And incidentally it was over-seasoned—that doesn't make you good father material!'

'I never said I'd make a good father—how can anybody know what sort of parent they'll make? But I'm willing to give it my best shot. It's not a crime to be excited about the prospect of parenthood, Rowena, but I'm not stupid. Of *course* I know it's going to take a lot of adjustment. There's a world of difference between being realistic and being negative.'

This combination of reasoned argument and sarcasm was mostly wasted on Rowena, whose short-circuited brain hadn't managed to make sense of anything beyond 'excited'.

She gave her head a tiny puzzled shake as her bemused eyes met his. 'You're *excited* about having a baby…?'

A wary frown appeared between his brows as he nodded firmly. 'What did you expect me to be?'

Angry…annoyed, at least…maybe even appalled. 'I'd *love* to be excited,' she admitted wistfully. The outline of his strong features suddenly blurred as hot tears filled her eyes. She blinked rapidly to stop them overflowing.

'What's stopping you?' he prompted, his anger fading away to nothing as she raised her luminous, tragic eyes to his. For once Rowena couldn't hide the conflict that was tearing her apart from the inside out.

'I can't…' She gulped. 'I'm too s…scared.' A bitter little laugh escaped her aching throat. 'No, that's not true. Actually,' she admitted bluntly, 'I'm *terrified*. What if I can't do it? What if I'm a lousy mother?' Her voice shook as her deepest fears were revealed. 'Oh, I know everyone *thinks* I do everything well. You know why that is, don't you?'

Quinn shook his head, afraid to say or do anything that might make her retreat behind her defences once more.

'I never attempt anything I know I won't be brilliant at…'

'Except driving,' Quinn interceded lightly.

She sniffed ruefully. 'Except driving,' she agreed.

'It's a neat trick.'

Rowena nodded, her jaw set rigid to stop her chin wobbling as she swallowed the lump in her tight, aching throat.

'I may be a coward, but don't run away with the idea I'll let you have this baby, Quinn. I'd fight you every step of the way if you made me.'

'Why?'

Rowena blinked, confused as much by the peculiar expression in his eyes as the abrupt question. 'Well, obviously…because… because…'

Quinn took her by the shoulders and gave her a tiny shake. *'Because…?'*

'Because I want this baby.' Her eyes widened to their fullest extent when she realised what she had just said.

'Because your body clock's ticking louder? Because your hormones are overriding your common sense?'

'No!' she denied, fiercely resentful of his suggestions. 'I just want a baby.' A sense of wonder drifted over her face.

'*My* baby,' he said softly.

Without thinking Rowena nodded—that was a big part of it.

'I do…I *really* do.' It was scary to hear herself admit for the first time that her decision to have the baby had very little to do with hormones or a sense of moral responsibility. She'd hidden away from the simple truth behind terms like duty and responsibility, and she'd blamed it on her biology, but all along she'd wanted a baby—not just any baby, but one that was hers and Quinn's!

Despite this revelation, there were still some corners of conflict in her mind. Part of her still thought it was selfish for someone like her to want a baby.

Quinn's head went back as he released a deep sigh. *'At last!'* he breathed. He straightened up and eyed her with approval tinged by relief. 'It took you long enough.'

Her bewilderment deepened. 'I don't understand,' she faltered.

'Sure you do,' he denied warmly. 'It's not difficult. You want this baby, Rowena—*our* baby.' His eyes flared with satisfaction.

And that makes him happy? she thought. This was making less and less sense.

'A minute ago I wasn't a fit mother, and you wanted to take the baby away from me.' Her expression darkened at the memory and without his being aware of it her hands spread protectively over her belly.

A fresh unpleasant possibility occurred to her. 'People will say my life is empty,' she wailed. 'That I can't get anyone to love me and that's why I'm having a baby.' Maybe they had a point?

Oh, God, what was she doing, saying these things to Quinn? He was probably taking notes for his lawyer.

The problem was, now that she'd finally started saying what she was feeling, she couldn't seem to close the floodgates. Like the copious tears she was continually brushing from her cheeks, the words just kept flowing.

'Do you think there's a possibility you've been reading your own copy too often…?'

'I'm perfectly serious!' she snapped.

'I know, that's what's so scary,' he muttered. 'Or, then again, perhaps they'll think the baby's the ultimate fashion accessory…?' he observed slyly.

Eyes wide with shocked indignation, her head reared back. She grunted and released her breath in a rueful sigh the second she encountered the wry expression in his heavy-lidded eyes. 'You have a very warped sense of humour,' she said. It occurred to her that Quinn seemed to be less shocked by her revelations than she was.

'Perhaps, but in a long line of extremely stupid things you've said recently that had to be one of the most stupid. There are a lot of people out there who love you, Rowena Parrish. You know that.'

'I know that,' she admitted shamefaced, thinking of her family who were even now probably worried sick about her. There was a little ache in her heart because if Quinn had wanted to add himself to the list he referred to he had surely just had the ideal opportunity.

His silence spoke volumes.

'If you were as lacking in maternal instincts as you make out you'd have jumped at the opportunity to palm off the baby and not turned all feral on me.' He rubbed the area mid-way up his chest where her aggressive finger had left a red patch that would later become a bruise.

'I didn't turn *feral*,' Rowena denied, embarrassed at the description. A flicker of shock crossed her face. 'Did you say that thing—about taking the baby—deliberately, to get a reaction?' she asked, not sure she liked the idea of him manipulating her in such a calculating manner.

'I wish I could claim to be that perceptive, but actually I just lost my cool. It's pretty hard when someone you care for is acting as if you've ruined their life—especially when it's a pretty justified viewpoint,' he brooded darkly.

For a brief moment Rowena flirted with the idea of challenging him about the 'someone you care for' content of his statement, but on sober reflection she decided to leave well alone. Leaping on some casual comment smacked of sad desperation, so instead she summoned up a strained smile.

'I suppose that's something; it's bad enough talking to you at the best of times. If you suddenly developed the ability to see into my head too… Well, it just doesn't bear thinking about!' she admitted frankly. Especially when you considered the erotic fantasies swirling about in her head!

'Sometimes,' he replied, catching the angle of her jaw between his thumb and forefinger, 'I think I do know what you're thinking and on those occasions it seems spookily like you know what I'm thinking too… Let's try out the theory. What am I thinking now?' he asked throatily.

Rowena caught her breath. His expression was still and tense and inside all that stillness his wonderful eyes glowed. They had that dark, raw, turned on look that made her melt inside and turned her control switch all the way to frantic!

She licked her lips nervously and swayed towards him, completely mesmerised. He had barely even touched her and in a matter of seconds she was totally out of control. She wanted him to touch her, though; she wanted it badly.

Her heart rate would have set cardiac monitors screaming warnings, her skin temperature shot up several degrees. She was so aroused that every slight movement, the very touch of the air on her skin made her shift restlessly.

'Well…?'

This was the point where she could easily have cooled things down with a few well-chosen words. Instead of using those words she heard herself respond in an embarrassingly weak, breathless whisper.

'I really…I really couldn't say.'

'I'm thinking about your hair.' His voice had the texture of rough velvet as he reached out and let a few soft strands of her pale hair slide through his long fingers. 'So silky, so fine.' Rowena shivered and did so again and again as uncontrollable tremors slid through her body. 'And your skin, so smooth and firm like satin.' One finger trailed down her cheek before falling away. His darkened eyes fell at the same moment to the agitated rise and fall of her unconstrained breasts under the borrowed sweater.

When his eyes lifted they were burning. It was just a look but her insides flooded with hot pleasure and even hotter desire—she was on fire for him. She whimpered with relief when he took her face between his hands and drew her pliant body towards him.

'Are you going to kiss me any time soon?' she asked, looking from his eyes to his mouth and back again.

'All in good time,' he purred, running his tongue over the inside of her full, pouting lower lip.

Anticipating the actual moment he would eventually possess the honeyed sweetness of her lips only heightened the desire coursing like fire through his veins. However, this small display of will-power gave him the illusion he still had some control, some choice, but deep down Quinn knew that where Rowena was concerned his discipline was nil!

The bottom of her stomach dissolved. *'Oh, my God!'* Weak with need to the point of collapse, she clung to him. Her engorged nipples burned, the clutching, congested ache low in her belly reached crisis point as her firm, rounded thighs trembled.

Given the urgency of her need, this was not a moment for subtlety! Motivated now by nothing but a driving need to assuage the demanding ache centred between her legs, she pushed herself against him, rubbing her body erotically against the aggressive bulge of his hard arousal.

As she felt him suck in his breath Rowena pressed her open mouth to his. Quinn's response was immediate; he was kissing her back with a frantic hunger and wild intensity that made her senses spin. Like a famished man, his tongue plunged and tasted, his teeth nipped—it was more than a kiss but less than total possession, and Rowena wanted total possession!

Her neck extended to give his mouth access to the smooth, graceful curve. 'Take me to bed?' she whispered as his breath fanned over her ear. Eyes burning, she turned her face to his.

Quinn's face was very close to hers. She had time to hazily note that there was a dark flush along his cheekbones and the angular planes of his face appeared harder and sharper in the moment before his piercing eyes captured her own. After that she couldn't see anything but those glorious emerald depths.

'See, I told you, you do know what I'm thinking.' He grinned, sweeping her up into his arms.

When Rowena woke some time later darkness had fallen; the candles in the wall sconces flickered, sending dancing, elongated shadows across the crumpled bedclothes and the two occupants.

Yawning, she stretched languidly, with an almost feline grace, and her knee came into contact with something solid and warm. Shocked into wakefulness, she jerked back, her blue eyes shot open—then she relaxed. It was Quinn.

Who else did you expect? she asked herself mockingly.

Rowena had never woken up beside a man, never watched a man sleep, and the unexpected intimacy of this warm, sleepy afterglow took her by surprise.

Head supported on one hand, she looked curiously at the man beside her. He lay asleep on his stomach, his head turned to one side with the heavy, decadent, embroidered velvet top cover pushed down to his waist. The soft golden candlelight flickered over the powerful sculpted contours of his back and brought out the subtle auburn highlights in his dark, glossy hair. His even-coloured golden skin looked satiny and smooth.

He appeared to be sleeping deeply, the rhythm of his breathing deep and regular, his head cradled in the crook of one arm. In slumber his stern profile was softer, almost vulnerable. Looking at the strong, clean-cut lines of his jaw, the droop of heavy lashes across his slashing cheekbone, made her feel almost protective—or was it almost possessive…?

No almost about it, girl! The thought of any other woman being where she was, seeing what she was seeing, made her sick with jealousy. It was an emotion she'd never experienced in relation to a male before, and the raw intensity of it scared her.

Would he wake if she touched him? Her fingertips flexed as she silently contemplated tracing the line of his strong, supple spine all the way down to that intriguing cleft just above his tight buttocks. The texture, taste and scent of that smooth olive-toned skin was still fresh in her head. A small, gloating smile tugged at full lips still tender and swollen from his kisses as she thought about rediscovering the tactile delights his body offered.

Quinn shifted restlessly in his sleep and Rowena drew guiltily back, and then she drew back some more as he rolled even closer in the big bed. She bit back a startled cry as, with an indistinct, throaty murmur, he threw his arm over her body.

She lay there hardly daring to move, hardly daring to breathe. His arm heavy, inert and warm lay just below her ribcage, effectively pinning her to the bed. Well, this wasn't strictly true—she *could* have moved, it was more a case of she didn't want to! She shot a darting glance to his long fingers curled possessively over the crest of her hip and a flash-flood of heat engulfed her body.

Slowly, concentrating on a small portion of her body at a time she forced herself to relax. It wasn't as if it was a *bad* feeling having his warm body close to her, so close in fact she could feel his breath on her neck.

Her own body still felt warm and satiated, the glow low in her belly a reminder of Quinn's ferociously tender possession.

Quinn had lit the candles before they'd made love.

'That settles it. *Definitely* a love-nest, no doubt whatsoever,' he announced authoritatively. 'Candles are a girl thing. The only reason a man uses candles is to put a lady in the right mood.'

'Speaking from personal experience, are we?' she mocked as she covetously watched the long, lean fluid lines of his body as he padded about with lithe, unselfconscious grace, lighting them all before the burning taper in his hand almost singed his fingertips.

'Have you burnt yourself? You should put them in water.'

'I've a much better idea,' Quinn replied, leaping onto the bed with athletic fervour. 'You lick them cool for me. Medically speaking, saliva has astonishing healing powers.'

This scandalous suggestion made her colour rise. 'That's a very resourceful suggestion,' she admitted hoarsely.

'I'm a very resourceful man.' The resourceful man started stripping off his trousers.

If she'd been feeling a little more assured Rowena might have challenged him to prove this claim. But she thought her response was pretty adequate—Quinn's reaction to it suggested it was, anyhow.

The complacent grin was certainly wiped off his face when, kneeling just in front of him, she whipped the borrowed jumper over her head and flung it carelessly aside.

His eyes and jaw dropped simultaneously.

'Oh, my God!' she heard him mutter.

Her eyes smouldered with sultry triumph as the air was audibly expelled from his lungs in one long, painful gasp. Surviving his scorching scrutiny without covering herself or moving was a feat of remarkable endurance. Eventually she could bear it no more.

'Which hand was it?'

His glazed, unfocused gaze returned jerkily to her face. 'To hell with hands!' he growled, lunging for her.

The memory of what came next she would treasure for the rest of her life. His erotic explorations made her skin burn. And when it came the climax surpassed the mere physical—it touched her soul. In fact it did more than that:it provided proof positive for a born cynic that she had one!

Maybe some of what she felt communicated itself to Quinn because he didn't question the tears that poured down her cheeks as he drew her into his arms afterwards.

'Why are you crying?'

The sound of his voice in the present made Rowena start violently. Awkwardly she edged farther down beneath the covers and drew them up over her bare shoulders.

'I didn't know you were awake.' She hadn't known she was crying either. She touched the back of her hand to her cheek and felt the moisture.

'I'm about half and half.' Quinn rolled onto his back and stretched luxuriously, one arm flung over his head.

'Are you going to tell me why…?'

Rowena, conscious that she had been all but drooling at the rippling display of muscular perfection, withdrew her flustered glance and shook her head. 'Hmm?'

'You might recall I asked you why you're crying a whole sixty seconds ago,' came the wry reminder.

Considering he was responsible for her lack of concentration, she didn't think it very nice of him to be irritated by it.

'Oh, that.' She shrugged, dismissing the tears. 'I wasn't crying, I was just thinking about…' She dropped her eyes self-consciously. She could hardly tell him his ardent lovemaking was so spectacularly unforgettable—so uniquely fulfilling that the memory would probably still be able to reduce her to an emotional basket case when she was an old, old lady.

'About something that made you cry?' Suspicion threaded his words.

She rubbed her nose against the sheet. 'What can I say? I'm a mess of seething hormones.' The comment invited laughter but Quinn didn't seem to realise it; his expression remained sombre and thoughtful.

'I suppose you are.' A man would have to be very insensitive to ask a woman whose hormones were all over the show to make a life-changing decision.

Abruptly he rolled onto his stomach and planted a hand either side of her face on the pillow. There was nothing in any way lecherous about his lazy, warm smile but her heart began to race. But then the scent of his skin in her nostrils was enough to do that and you couldn't discount the degree to which the brazen pressure of his heavy thigh against her own disconcerted her!

Rowena swallowed convulsively—he was so damned gorgeous she couldn't take her eyes off him.

He looked down at the outline of her slim body lying beneath him. A frown appeared above his aquiline nose as his roaming glance reached the suggestion of soft hips under the covers and stayed put. 'I take it your gynaecologist has not picked up any problems?' he probed cautiously.

'I'm pregnant, not ill, Quinn.'

Quinn looked exasperated by her impatient response. 'In other words you've not seen a doctor yet.' He sighed, shaking his head. 'That's so typical of you, Parrish.'

'I've seen you.' Suppressing a bubble of naughty laughter, she caught her lower lip between her teeth. 'Quite a lot of you actually, *Tyler*,' she elaborated with a lascivious little leer as her glance followed the flow of dark body hair on his chest to the place where it arrowed into a thin fine line over his lean belly. The image sent an excited shiver down her spine. 'And very nice too,' she admitted, a husky catch in her voice.

'Very kind of you to say so.'

She reached up and let her fingers slide across his collar-bone. A slow, sultry smile tugged at her wide, sexy mouth.

'You know,' she mused throatily, 'I think I might be passably good at it after all. It as in sex, and passably as in pretty marvellous.'

Quinn raised himself above her and supported himself on straight arms. After his initial sharp inhalation his breathing seemed to have settled into a shallow, almost laboured pattern.

'You wouldn't be trying to distract me, would you?'

At this point Rowena, who was regretting her brazen behaviour, would have liked to turn away, but breaking eye contact with Quinn when he had other ideas was a non-starter.

'You haven't told me what you think.'

'I think,' he finally responded in a low, sardonic drawl, 'that it isn't outside the realms of possibility. In fact, given the right encouragement, I think you could be *brilliant*.' He shook his head as a slow grin split his dark features. 'Though I have to admit you're doing pretty well just doing what comes naturally.' With a laugh he suddenly rolled away from her.

Rowena found herself laughing too as they lay side by side staring at the rich canopy over their heads. Almost in unison they turned their heads to face one another. Continuing the symmetrical theme, the laughter died from both their faces at the same moment—the moment that the electricity flashed between them.

As if drawn by an invisible cord, Rowena leaned towards him, bringing her face close up to his.

'Come on, 'fess up, Rowena, you haven't seen a doctor, have you?'

A sound of frustration whistled through her teeth as she angrily rolled herself in the sheet and to the opposite side of the bed. Her *femme fatale* act obviously needed some work. Talk about anticlimax!

'I've hardly had time yet to see doctors,' she said crossly.

'That's no excuse—it's been over two months since the baby was conceived. It's *always* possible to make time for the important things in life,' he evangelised virtuously.

Virtue, she reflected grumpily, was so much harder to stomach when you knew the person dishing it out was right.

'What sort of things would those be, Quinn?' she asked, displaying deep interest. 'Being seen at film premières with bosomy starlets?'

Quinn grimaced. 'Ah, you saw that one, did you?'

'Holly sent me the video tape.' At the time she had wondered why her sister had imagined that seeing Quinn for thirty seconds parading through a foyer of celebrities with a skimpily dressed actress on his arm would offer any entertainment value.

'Actually, Angie wasn't really *that* well endowed. It was just an unfortunate camera angle and a lot of, erm, *underwiring*...' He shifted his weight onto one elbow and used his other hand to mime the uplift aspect of his description.

Rowena sniffed with lofty disdain. 'Unfortunate from whose point of view?'

'I was simply doing a mate a favour, you know.'

She smiled understandingly. 'And hating every minute of it, I could tell,' she guffawed insincerely.

'Mark, the poor sod, had mumps. He was totally gutted; he'd been chasing Angie for months. He had enough to worry about with the spectre of infertility hanging over him without imagining some smoothie running off with his girlfriend.'

And this from the smoothie of all smoothies!

'And he thought you were a safe pair of hands? My, doesn't he need his head testing!'

Quinn's fascinating mouth twitched. 'As illuminating as this display of claws is, I think we're drifting again…' He didn't allow Rowena, who had opened her mouth to hotly contest this accusation of jealousy, to get a word in before he seamlessly continued. 'The first thing we do when we get back to London is organise some antenatal care for you. I know a really first-class woman, Alex Stone, you'd get on with her…but of course if you have someone else in mind…'

'You mean I can actually choose my own doctor?' She gasped, giving her best rendering of a helpless little girl voice. 'Are you quite sure?'

'Very funny. But, seriously, Rowena, we shouldn't drag our feet on this one—'

'We?'

'Of course *we*. I want to be with you every step of the way with this, Rowena, before and after the birth. And while we're talking about it, this might be as good a time as any to think about the benefits of us moving in together?'

He looked and sounded so damned *casual* that Rowena's first thought was that she must have misunderstood him.

'You're suggesting that we move in together?'

'It would make child care a lot easier—think about it…' he suggested, hardly sounding as if her decision was exactly life or death to him. 'There's no desperate hurry, but I think you'll find it makes sense,' he added, levering himself upright and throwing back the covers, displaying a relaxed attitude to his naked state that Rowena frankly envied.

Sense!

The argument no longer had the same pulling power for her that it had done until recently. No, Rowena had discovered she wasn't so different from her contemporaries after all. She didn't want sense, she wanted *passion*! She wanted a man who said his life would be nothing without her in it; she wanted promises of eternal devotion—in short, she wanted the full works!

And Quinn very obviously wasn't going to supply them. There was a certain horrid irony to the situation. Rowena, who had spent her life avoiding emotional complications, had fallen for a guy who had an approach as pragmatic as her own had been.

Still, you couldn't throw the baby out with the bath water...a flicker of affection closely followed by worry crossed her face as she heard Gran's brisk, no-nonsense voice in her head serving up this favourite piece of advice. It was one she had frequently employed when Rowena had been on the point of ditching some scheme or other that hadn't gone exactly to plan.

It wasn't exactly hard to think of plus points beyond the mere practicality of living with Quinn when he was strutting about the bedroom in a state of beautiful undress. And who was to say his feelings wouldn't deepen later?

Rowena, the covers modestly drawn around her shoulders, sat upright. The defiant tilt of her chin was aimed more at the small voice in her head that despaired at the unrealistic, fingers-crossed decision she'd arrived at with such undue haste than at him.

'All right, then.'

'All right?' Quinn paused in the act of retrieving his trousers from the floor—not a situation that would show off most men to their best advantage, but then Quinn was not your average man!

She watched him straighten up with that smooth, fluid grace that typified his every movement; her stomach responded quiveringly to the striking erotic image.

'On one condition.'

'We are talking about us moving in together, here, aren't we?'

Rowena nodded. Unusually for Quinn, he was displaying shock—perhaps at the speed with which she'd reached her decision.

'I think we should have a probationary period during which we can find out if we're compatible,' she said, trying with her aloof demeanour to rebalance any appearance of undesirable eagerness she might have previously displayed.

'We know we're perfectly compatible.' His eyes moved extremely obviously in the direction of the tumbled bed covers, inescapable evidence of their frantic coupling.

If sex was all it took to make a successful relationship, they'd have it made, she thought, removing her own gaze from the proof of their lovemaking. 'I'm talking about outside the bedroom,' she snapped back.

'Two seconds.'

Her frown deepened. 'Two seconds what?'

'It took seconds for your blush to peak.'

'You were timing it?'

He nodded. 'That might be a record.'

'I'm awfully glad I amuse you.' This was only their future she was talking about and he was making dumb jokes at her expense.

Quinn sighed. 'It's only a joke. I like you blushing. It's charming and cute.'

'Cute!' she echoed, her face screwed up in disgust. 'Is that meant to be a compliment? If so, I have to tell you, you badly miscalculated.'

Quinn's jaw tightened. 'Perhaps you should compile a blacklist of unacceptable compliments.'

How did he always turn things around so that she came out the unreasonable one? 'You wouldn't call a man cute, would you?' Not the most staggeringly intelligent riposte you've ever come up with, Rowena, she told herself.

'You don't want me to answer that, do you?'

Rowena shook her head, feeling a complete moron. 'But I do want you to treat me like your intellectual equal, not someone to pat on the head.'

'So I'm supposed to say your intellect turns me on? Well, quite frankly I'd be lying. Your mind is a maze to me, your motivations are mostly a complete mystery, I just think I've got you worked out and you go and—'

'Do something daft and get pregnant.'

'There you go again!' he yelled as, pushing his fingers deep into his dark hair, he shook his head wearily from side to side. 'Putting words into my mouth. For heaven's sake, woman, why can't you just go with the flow?' He sighed.

With an inarticulate squeal of frustration Rowena grabbed a pillow and pushed her head under it.

It was hard to maintain his animosity when confronted by the image of her neat little behind stuck up in the air, swaying gently backwards and forwards.

When her repertoire of foul language was exhausted Rowena emerged, her cheeks pink and her hair sticking up.

'Have you *any* idea how much you irritate me when you say things like that?' she demanded.

'Things like what?'

'Chill out, go with the flow…' With a choked sob she pulled the pillow across her chest and buried her face in it. She stayed like that for several moments, rocking back and fro before straightening up. 'Well, any trial run seems obsolete now, doesn't it?'

Quinn folded his arms across his bare chest and looked belligerent. 'Why's that?'

'Are you *mad*? We've got nothing whatever in common. The fact is I'm a picture straightener, always have been, always will be, and you...' She forced herself to look at the tall, dynamic figure who made her ache with a mixture of lust, love and frustration. 'At heart you're a slob, Quinn. Oh, I know you look respectable when you're working.' Respectable hardly covered the elegant, commanding figure he cut in his dark designer suits and handmade shoes. 'But that's not the real you, is it?'

'You think you know who the real me is?' He looked fascinated.

'The real you is the one crawling round underneath that motorbike of yours wearing jeans and a tee shirt covered in oil.'

'Well, I'd look damned stupid fixing the brake pads on the bike in a suit and tie, wouldn't I?'

'You're missing the point.'

'No, I'm not, you're getting bogged down with a lot of stupid details that don't really matter. The bottom line is your life has improved beyond all recognition with me in it.'

A laugh of pure disbelief was torn from her throat. 'You really are unbelievable!' She gasped, half laughing at his outrageous arrogance.

'It's true, you've always needed a challenge—'

'I can't dispute you're that!'

'Your trouble is you inspire admiration, awe and fear in men.'

'But not in you?'

'No, when I'm not wanting to strangle you, I'm thinking about when, where and how I'm going to make love to you,' he announced with breathtaking candour.

All manner of steamy images passed rapidly before her burning eyes as she drew in a shuddering breath.

'Always supposing we did move in together, and I'm only saying *supposing*…' she began shakily.

'Of course.'

She was relieved to see he was happy to play along with the pretence that her decision hadn't always been a foregone conclusion.

She'd been making sensible decisions all her life—perhaps it was time she started making the odd crazy one. She was starting to think that steering clear of emotional attachments hadn't been sensible, just cowardly. Or maybe there was only so long you could ignore your genes—perhaps it was her destiny to go crazy like all the other women in her family.

'There's another condition,' she explained, trying to give the impression this codicil was an unimportant afterthought.

Quinn looked suspicious. 'You don't want me to sell my bike, do you?'

She shook her head. 'I don't think we should date anyone else.' She half expected him to pick up on the inescapable fact there wasn't much possibility of her *pulling* with a bump the size of a house preceding her into a room!

'Monogamy?' Quinn sucked in his breath and shook his head doubtfully. 'That's a big ask!'

Rowena's heart dropped somewhere south of her knees; her stomach churned. If her eyes hadn't also dropped she'd have recognised the unmistakable flare of anger in Quinn's lustrous eyes.

'It's non-negotiable,' she gritted. Compromise was one thing, becoming a doormat was something else again.

'Good grief, woman!' Quinn ejaculated, his expression morphing into one of extreme exasperation as his green eyes skimmed her flushed face. 'Do you actually think I'm the sort of man who would have one woman at home and keep a bit on the side?' He looked at her expression of self-conscious guilt and snorted with disgust. 'Oh, that's just damned great,' he drawled with a jaundiced scowl. 'You do, don't you?'

Rowena's eyes slid uncomfortably away from the accusation in his cynical glare. 'I just wanted you to know what you were letting yourself in for,' she muttered, chewing her lip.

'It would seem I'm letting myself in for living with a woman who thinks I have no staying power in the fidelity department.'

'It's not too late to change your mind!' she flared.

Quinn's narrowed gaze stilled on her flushed face. 'Oh, you'll not get rid of me that easily, sweetheart.'

Rowena shivered. 'You make it sound like a threat,' she accused, secretly relieved he hadn't taken her up on her rash offer.

It was quite horrifically politically incorrect to be attracted by the air of danger he was effortlessly projecting, but she couldn't help herself. Perhaps, she pondered, it was all right to be turned on by menace when you knew the person oozing it would never hurt you.

Quinn smiled and pulled the narrow-cut trousers up over his snaky hips. 'A threat, a promise.' He shrugged carelessly. 'It's much the same thing.'

A promise, she thought, didn't have sinister overtones.

'All this quarrelling doesn't seem a very auspicious start to this...this...' What did you call what they were embarking on? She glanced up at Quinn who had obviously recognised her dilemma and had no intention of helping her out. '*Arrangement,*' she finished with a sigh of relief.

'People in *arrangements* frequently quarrel, Rowena, though I can hardly expect you to know about such things.'

'*Meaning...?*'

'Meaning you've got a nerve questioning my commitment. If you recall, it was me who wanted to put our relationship on a more formal footing right from the beginning—you were the one that wanted the freedom to shop around.'

The crude assessment made her wince. 'Just how many lovers do you think I've had?' she yelled. 'I have never *shopped around*, as you put it, and you can't pretend that you would have been talking about moving in together if I hadn't got pregnant.'

'We'll never know, will we?'

Rowena knew evasion when she heard it.

'And the point is you *are* pregnant. Let's deal with that.'

Rowena took a deep breath. He was right. She had to deal with the knowledge that she loved someone who didn't love her. It's not a total tragedy, she told herself sternly. Stop griping about what you don't have and wake up to what you do have—Quinn is a fantastic lover, he'll make a great father to our child and he'll never deliberately hurt you.

'Yes, and a baby needs security.' Not to mention two parents.

An odd expression flickered into Quinn's eyes. 'And what do you need, Rowena?'

Love! she wanted to shout.

Fortunately the emotional lump the size of a large boulder that was at that moment lodged in her aching throat ruled out such an indiscreet and unwise response. Mutely she shook her head.

'I know right now it feels as if you're giving up your freedom, but you never know—one day you might even come to believe you'd gained something even more precious.'

Leaving her to ponder his cryptic parting shot, he pushed open the door of the *en suite* bathroom and strode inside, the door clicking closed after him.

Rowena had just started tidying away the remains of the meal Quinn had cooked when he appeared wearing a towel around his trim middle.

'What are you doing?'

Despite the fact it must be perfectly obvious what she was doing, in the interests of harmony Rowena replied, 'Clearing up.'

'Leave it until later,' Quinn responded, dismissing the sink half full of dirty pots with a lordly gesture.

'But...but...' Her eyes widened as Quinn snuffed out the candles she'd lit between his thumb and forefinger.

'Now you can't see them. Does that make it easier?' His dark velvet voice reached her through the blanket of darkness.

'I'll still know they're there.'

She started as his hand closed firmly over hers. 'Listen, I think I'm taking it pretty well considering you obviously find it hard to choose between me and dirty dishes. So stop fussing, woman, and come with me.'

'Come where? I can't see,' she protested, resisting just enough to demonstrate she wasn't a pushover, but not enough to discourage him too much as he tugged her forward.

'I'll see for us both.'

'Oh, and I suppose you can see in the dark?'

'Actually I do happen to have exceptional night vision…'

'And an ego the size of Ben Nevis,' she grumbled as an iron arm fastened around her waist. 'It doesn't look as if I have much choice, does it?'

'And we all know how much you *love* to sit back and let someone else take control.'

Frowningly, she absorbed his smooth comment as he led her across the room and to the foot of the stairs without bumping into anything. It was either luck or it hadn't been an idle boast—he really could see in the dark.

'Are you saying I'm a control freak?' she demanded as they mounted the stairs together.

Quinn laughed bitterly in reply but didn't pause. He led her swiftly through the bedroom and towards the bathroom.

Rowena tried to wrest her arm from his tenacious grip. 'Will you just let me—?'

'Stop it, you'll hurt yourself.'

'No, actually, *you'll* hurt me…'

With a curse Quinn released her arm.

'Thank you,' she began sarcastically.

Quinn leant over her head and pushed the bathroom door behind her open. Her head automatically turned in the direction of the soft light that suddenly spilled from the room. *'Oh, wow!'* she breathed, stepping like someone in a dream over the threshold.

The opulent room with its enormous claw-footed bath was filled with the light of flickering candles; they covered just about every available surface. The soft light picked out the fragrant oil floating on the warm water filling the tub. If there had ever been a seduction scene set, she was looking at it.

She heard the door softly close.

'You did this for me?' she whispered, not turning around.

His hands moved to her shoulders, drawing her back against his body. 'I did this for us, Rowena,' he corrected throatily. 'I'd like us to take some good memories away with us.'

Tears standing out in her eyes, she spun around. 'Oh, Quinn,' she cried, 'I've already got more of those than I ever thought possible!' she declared passionately.

'There's room for more, though...?'

She reached boldly for the zip on his trousers. 'Definitely,' she agreed, her eyes not leaving his.

CHAPTER EIGHT

QUINN heard the sound of barking and straightened up. He flexed his shoulders to ease the ache between his shoulder blades and thrust the shovel he'd been wielding for the last half-hour into the snow. Despite the beginnings of a thaw there was no shortage of that.

The dog he'd heard reached him before the group of men who were just beyond hailing distance. Quinn waved a hand at them before squatting down to stroke the animal frisking affectionately around his feet.

'Are you the rescue party, boy?' he asked, running his fingers through the collie's glossy coat. 'Clever boy,' he approved. 'In fact, I've known hospital managers that look less intelligent than you—a lot less,' he added as he looked into the bright, intelligent eyes of the dog.

The animal, detecting a note of praise in the man's deep voice, barked some more and wagged his tail enthusiastically.

Hearing the tramp of human feet, Quinn pulled himself upright and, brushing the snow from his knees, prepared to meet his rescue party, who would no doubt think he was a total bloody fool to abandon the relative safety of a car in the middle of a blizzard. He steeled himself for their scorn.

At an educated guess he suspected the well-equipped group approaching were members of a local mountain rescue team, or something similar. Oh, well, he reflected philosophically, at least they were accustomed to dealing with reckless fools as well as the genuinely unfortunate.

'Saw the smoke,' the chap walking in the front of the party called, gesturing towards the chimney stack. He peeled back the ear flaps from his cap and brushed a few stray flakes of snow from his rusty-coloured beard. 'We were wondering if you know anything about the silver Saab down on the road? The hire company's got it registered to a…Miss…'

'Rowena Parrish,' Quinn supplied as the bearded chap ransacked his pockets for the relevant piece of paper. 'We're together,' he added.

The leader, left with the immediate impression it would take a person of unusual determination or spectacular foolishness to separate this man from the woman in question, nodded. A man of few words himself, he appreciated the tall guy's ability to say more with two words than most people managed with several dozen.

'She's all right?'

Quinn nodded. 'Inside, straightening things up. We were going to try and make it out a little later.'

'Let Headquarters know, Jack,' he instructed one of his companions. 'We're from the local mountain rescue, we're helping out the emergency services. Ralf MacNeil…' He extended his gloved hand.

A manly handshake was exchanged as Quinn too identified himself.

'The snowplough hasn't got this far yet, but we can give you a lift in the off-roader as far as the motel on the main road. That's where most of the other stranded folk ended up before.'

'Those that didn't leave their cars,' Quinn put in drily.

'Not the best idea…'

Quinn appreciated the tact of his politely restrained reply. 'Incidentally, how far away is the car? We lost all sense of direction,' he admitted.

'About five hundred yards over that ridge,' one of the younger men responded, pointing in the direction they'd just come from.

Quinn laughed and shook his head. 'We probably weren't any farther than that from it the whole time. We were walking round in circles.' Irony didn't get much darker than dying of exposure yards away from your own car, but as Quinn wasn't the sort of man to waste his time worrying about things that hadn't happened he didn't have a problem dismissing it from his mind.

'Snow can be very disorientating.'

'It's not the only thing,' Quinn responded, thinking of the infuriating woman inside. The other man looked puzzled but Quinn didn't fill in the blanks. 'Come in and I'll break the good news to Rowena.'

Rowena, who had tried to return the cottage to its original pristine condition, received the news of their rescue with mixed feelings, which she tried hard not to show.

It wasn't that she didn't want to leave—of course she did, she was desperate to get the hospital—but she couldn't resist a few wistful backward glances at the cottage as the team of mountaineers led them back to civilisation. Sealed away from the world, for a short blissful time the pressures had ceased to exist. She wondered uneasily if they'd ever be able to regain that precious sense of harmony once they had to start juggling all the other demands of their lives.

Quinn caught her arm as she stumbled. 'It might be a good idea to look where you're going.' He intercepted the direction of her glance. 'You know, I'm quite going to miss the old place, too.'

'No electricity, no phone and no mod cons…I always knew you were odd, Quinn,' she scoffed pragmatically.

He brought his face down close to hers, close enough for her to appreciate the clear, close-textured qualities of his olive skin, close enough to affect her breathing, close enough to make her want to curl her fingers in his dark hair and tug him the extra inch or so until their lips were touching.

'I was thinking more about the company,' he purred. 'It's true you've got a mean streak, but I can't think of anyone else I'd prefer to be stranded in a snowstorm with.'

Bathed by the warmth of his gaze, Rowena was suddenly hit by a wave of incapacitating shyness.

'You did leave our phone numbers on that note?' she asked him, abruptly changing the subject.

Quinn didn't try and prevent her as she pulled away from him. 'I've already told you, phone number, address, e-mail and fax. Mind you, if you'd let me go through that desk we'd know who to contact,' he pointed out.

'The desk was locked,' she retorted, increasing her pace in the hope the exertion would help clear her befuddled senses. 'Anyhow, you can't rifle willy-nilly through other people's personal papers. Besides, all we have to do is ask the police to let the owner know what happened and he can contact us.'

Quinn shrugged. 'Have it your own way.'

Rowena sent him an irritated glare and hurried ahead to catch up the man who appeared to be in charge of the rescue.

She tapped him on the shoulder. 'Excuse me,' she panted. 'But I was wondering, do you think we'll be able to get through to Inverness later today?'

'I shouldn't think so.' A man more at ease with mountains than beautiful woman, he responded with restraint and avoided too much eye contact. However, his reserve cracked when he saw her face fall. Awkwardly he patted her on the back. 'Important, was it?'

Rowena nodded. 'My grandmother's ill, she's in hospital there.'

His craggy features softened. 'Ah, well, you might be able to get back to Glasgow.'

Rowena managed a polite smile. The man was only being helpful, but she didn't see there was much point in getting even farther away from her desired destination.

'And from there you could catch a flight up to Inverness.'

Later that night Ralf MacNeil told the barman at the Nag's Head that the lassie's smile had been like the sun breaking out.

'Why didn't I think of that…the airport has reopened?'

'I believe so.'

'Thank you, that's what I'll do.' When Quinn caught her up a few moments later she didn't share the information with him. It would be nice to show him after her feeble display so far that she was actually capable of organising things without his help.

*   *   *

Rowena unfastened her seat belt as the last leg of her journey finally came to an end.

A person accustomed to her own company, she had been startled to find herself on several occasions during the tedious but uneventful journey automatically turning to Quinn to share some snippet of information—not big, world-shattering stuff, just little things that she knew would make him smile, things like the big, butch-looking chap, obviously terrified of flying, who had been clinging to his delicate-looking girlfriend's hand for dear life ever since they took off.

Quinn hadn't been there most of her life so why did she experience that odd, empty feeling each time she recognised her solitary state now…?

She had no reason to feel guilty, she reminded herself as she disembarked. It wasn't as if she had to ask Quinn's permission before she made a decision.

It was questionable if Quinn would believe it, but she really hadn't *deliberately* set out to give him the slip. Though the breathing space to sort her thoughts out had been a definite plus point, she told herself, ignoring the fact that, though she'd done a lot of thinking during her solo journey north, none of it had been particularly constructive.

If Quinn hadn't pulled a vanishing act, if he'd actually been around when the talkative chap at the motel bar had offered her the spare seat in his minibus as far as Glasgow, he'd probably have told her to go for it. After all, that was what this journey had been all about, her getting to Gran—sure, a few unscheduled matters had come up along the way. She veered her thoughts away from those other matters and into safer channels, but it wasn't long before she was thinking about Quinn again.

What had he thought when the barman had given him the quick note of explanation she'd scribbled? The barman had promised faithfully to pass it on and in this instance Quinn's eye-catching qualities had come in very handy when she'd tried to describe him.

'You mean the tall, dark guy that brunette was all over.'

She wished that Quinn were there to hear this neutral assessment, which happened to coincide with her own. When she had casually mentioned something along these lines to Quinn he had had the cheek to infer she was jealous. The brunette, he'd said, was just *being friendly*.

'So friendly she was one step away from slipping you her room key!' Rowena had been provoked into responding.

It wasn't long after that he had vanished without a word of explanation. If she was the pathologically jealous type he implied, she might have thought he had gone to continue his *conversation* with the brunette.

'He's the one,' she confirmed grimly to the barman. 'I'd tell my friend myself,' she explained, 'but I don't know where he's got to, and they're leaving straight away.'

The barman tucked the note in his breast pocket. 'Don't you worry, I'll give him the message.'

Still she hovered. Nobody looking at her would have believed her decisiveness was one quality that every employer she'd ever had had raved about, she reflected with self-derision as she stood there torn, not knowing what to do for the best.

'We're off now if you're coming, love.'

Rowena made one last desperate search for the tall, dark, easily distinguishable head before she finally straightened her shoulders and nodded.

'Yes, please.'

And the journey had gone without a hitch if you discounted the fact the members of the bowling club, a group of respectable over-sixties, had got a bit raucous after the stop at the pub, and to avoid seeming stand-offish she'd felt obliged to join in their powerful rendering of 'Speed Bonny Boat'.

Presumably Quinn now knew where she was.

What had he done when he'd discovered she'd gone on without him? she wondered. Where was he now? Not up to his ankles in depressing slush, I bet, she thought, looking down at her icy extremities mired in the slushy mess—nor queuing for a taxi, either. Quinn was one of those irritating people who never had a problem locating a taxi.

Had he gone straight back to London, maybe? Should she ring him, or wait for him to contact her? If they were a *real* couple such details would not occupy her thoughts this way—real couples were already part of each other's lives.

God, even though they'd known each other since university they were virtually strangers, she thought as her feelings continued to see-saw violently from one extreme to the other.

What was I thinking of, agreeing to move in with him...? Talk about a recipe for disaster. I'd give us a month, six weeks tops, she thought gloomily as the rashness of her decision hit home once again.

In five minutes' time she'd nearly convinced herself that there was nothing stopping them building a future together except her disinclination to accept compromise.

'This has to stop!'

The man who had been going to barge past her to the taxi that had just drawn up stepped hastily to one side to give her a clear path.

Rowena, who was blissfully unaware she had spoken out loud, smiled at this sweetly chivalrous display.

Holly was waiting for her at the swing doors of the hospital entrance.

'She really is all right?' Rowena asked, breaking free of her sister's tight hug. 'You weren't just trying to make me feel better on the phone?'

Holly grinned. 'Come and see for yourself. I should warn you, though, she's not what you'd call an *easy* patient.'

Rowena blinked as her sister's face swam in and out of focus. 'Can I sit down for a minute…?' she asked faintly. 'I feel a bit wobbly.'

'I'm not surprised after your nightmare journey. We were worried sick when we couldn't contact you, but we knew you wouldn't come to any harm with Quinn around.'

The strange little strangled laugh that emerged from Rowena's bloodless lips made Holly's gaze sharpen as she anxiously scanned her sister's pale face. She led her without further comment to one of the chairs in the foyer.

'Can I get you anything? A glass of water?'

Rowena lifted her head from between her knees. 'No, I'm fine,' she replied, summoning a shaky smile. 'It's just I've been so afraid I didn't dare let myself believe she would be all right.'

Holly took her hand and squeezed it. 'I know exactly what you mean—but it's more than that, though, isn't it?' she added, with the startling perspicacity she had an unnerving habit of displaying.

Part of Rowena desperately ached to confide the whole story to Holly right there and then—the pregnancy, Quinn, everything—but common sense intervened, so she didn't say, I'm pregnant, or even, I'm in love—this wasn't the time or place for confessions.

'I could do with a blood sugar boost. I haven't had anything to eat since breakfast.'

It was fairly obvious that Holly wasn't totally convinced by this explanation, but she didn't push it. 'Shall I get you a bar of chocolate or something?'

'That might be a good idea.'

Holly's short absence gave Rowena the chance to get some sort of grip on her emotions

'What should I expect with Gran?' she asked tentatively as they walked along the hospital corridors. 'Is her speech affected or…?'

'You'll find her just as sharp as ever,' Holly responded, anticipating the question her sister was too scared to come right out and ask. 'There's no intellectual impairment at all. She's had a left-sided stroke, so that means one half of her body—the opposite side—has been affected. Gran's been lucky, she's already regaining some motor function. I suppose the most obvious thing you'll see is her face.' She touched the side of her own smooth cheek. 'The corner of her mouth has dropped, which has given her a slight slur, but there is no dysphasia.'

'Talk English, Holly…? Me not doctor, me simple magazine editor…'

Holly grinned. 'Her speech has not been affected.'

Rowena soon discovered this was true.

'Well, you took your time getting here,' Elspeth observed tartly as her tall, willowy granddaughter walked through the door.

'Gran!' Rowena cried, rushing straight past her mother who was seated at the bedside. She sat beside the frail figure in the bed, tears streaming down her cheeks.

'Your mascara will run,' the old lady predicted.

'I'm not wearing any,' Rowena choked.

'No,' her sister mused gloomily, 'it's all natural. Doesn't it make you sick?' She sighed.

'It seems to me, Holly, you've found someone who likes you just the way you are.' Having reduced her younger granddaughter to blushing silence, she turned to the elder. 'For goodness' sake, girl, give me a hug. I won't break!'

Rowena glanced uncertainly at her mother, who nodded in encouragement.

'I'm so sorry I couldn't get here sooner, Gran.' Rowena sighed when she eventually drew back.

'No, you've been having quite an adventure, I understand, though I suspect I've been getting a strictly expurgated version from your man.'

'I...I don't understand...*my* man...?'

'Don't go all coy on me, Rowena.'

'I'm not being coy, Gran, I...'

Holly came to her rescue. 'She doesn't know Quinn is here, Gran, she hasn't seen him yet.'

No trace of colour in her face, Rowena spun around. 'Quinn is here? But that isn't possible!' she babbled. 'I caught the first plane up here and he was...'

'Cadging a lift off an old mate of his who runs a helicopter service.'

Wasn't that just typical of Quinn—he always had to go one better, was Rowena's first thought. The second was pure panic.

'That means that he's here in Inverness,' she said blankly.

She'd pictured him in his London flat, in the motel bar getting drunk and calling her names, even, but never in her wildest dreams had she pictured him here!

'Actually he's here in the hospital,' Holly said, regarding her shaken sister with sympathy tinged with a liberal dollop of curiosity.

'He and Niall have taken Dad and Gramps to the canteen for something to eat. They should be back any minute now.'

'Oh, God!' What, she wondered, furtively scrutinising the faces of her nearest and dearest, what had he been saying behind her back? 'I hope he hasn't been boring you…' she probed hopefully.

'Actually it was a relief to talk to someone who doesn't act like I'm about to keel over and die any second.'

'Yes, Quinn's a lovely man, Rowena,' her mother agreed in her soft voice.

'Not to mention indecently good-looking,' Holly added, grinning at Rowena.

Rowena found she couldn't grin back. She gulped. If she couldn't take a teasing remark off her sister, how was she going to cope with total strangers leering lustfully at him? Because they would. Quinn inspired a very high lust factor in women.

'You go along and meet them, girls, I want a nap—'

'I'll stay—' Rowena began.

'Nonsense, your mother will keep me company, won't you, Eileen?'

The sisters exchanged glances. They both knew that, ill or not, when Elspeth used *that* tone there was no point arguing.

'Do you want to go up to the canteen to see if they're still there?' Holly asked.

'Definitely not!' Rowena didn't know much but she knew that she wasn't in any hurry to confront Quinn.

'We got such a shock when he turned up without you, but when he explained how you'd gone and hitched a lift we all laughed—even Niall, *thank goodness*.'

'Oh, yes, hilarious,' Rowena gritted. Her smooth brow puckered and she stopped in the middle of the corridor. 'Why *even* Niall?' she queried sharply.

'Well, they haven't met since the last time…'

'And what happened the last time Niall and Quinn met?'

An expression of comical dismay tinged by embarrassment crossed her sister's face. 'He didn't tell you…I assumed…'

'Didn't tell me what?'

Holly sighed. 'I don't think he wanted me to tell you, Rowena…'

'I don't give a damn what he wants.'

Holly sighed. 'Well, the last time they met was one morning at your place—it was when you were in America, and Niall, well, Niall...'

'Niall what?' Rowena prompted, running out of patience.

'He hit Quinn—knocked him down, actually. Fortunately Quinn was feeling a bit "the morning after the night before", if you get my meaning, so there wasn't a full scale brawl or anything,' Holly confided ingenuously.

'Well, yes, that *was* lucky. How did Quinn and Niall both happen to be in my flat on the same morning?'

'Well, Quinn arrived the night before—'

'The night before?'

'Yeah, and he'd had a real skinful...I mean he was *really* drunk.'

'Quinn doesn't drink!' Rowena protested faintly.

'I don't know about that, but he had that night.'

'What did he do?'

'Well, actually, he got into your bed...'

'Which you were using?' Cold fear froze Rowena to the spot. No, he couldn't have...Holly wouldn't have...*not in my own bed*?

'Yes, I'd gone to London to see Niall and was using your place like I always do,' Holly, still blissfully unaware of the storm about to break over her innocent head, confirmed. 'And I didn't have the heart to pitch him out, poor love. The next morning Niall showed up just as Quinn was coming out of the shower and he sort of—'

'I think I get the picture,' Rowena responded, her lip curling in distaste, her stomach churning.

'Yes, well, you know Niall and how *irrational* he can be sometimes.' The thought of her fiancé and his numerous faults brought a soppy smile to her lips.

'Irrational…?' Rowena looked at her sister as if she'd never seen her before.

Take away the glorious mane of untamable red hair, the great body, the sinfully sexy mouth and what did you have that had men like Niall and Quinn making fools of themselves? she asked herself. If you discounted the fact she was feisty and funny—*nothing*!

'I think that under the circumstances you're lucky he's been so tolerant.'

'What?' Holly yelped, staring in shocked consternation into her lovely sister's eyes,

which were at that moment about as friendly as a sharpened scalpel.

'If you actually want to keep Niall, Holly,' Rowena added with a frigid smile of disdain, 'you'll mend your ways, because even if he is besotted Niall isn't the type of man to accept that sort of behaviour from his wife, and, quite frankly...' she wobbled, her superior sneer quivering into a look of unmitigated misery '...I think he deserves better!'

She turned sharply on her heel and left a flabbergasted Holly staring after the tall figure stalking away down the corridor.

Rowena had no idea where she was going. She just knew if she'd not removed herself the temptation to shake her sister until her teeth rattled would have been too difficult to resist. Holly had been so *casual* about it, that was the worst part, as though sleeping with the man her sister loved was no big deal. And as for Quinn—the rat, being as drunk as a skunk was no excuse in her mind for such an act of betrayal with *her own sister*!

Quinn, the great straight-talker; Quinn whose integrity she had taken pretty much for granted, had turned out to be the sort of man who would sleep with your best friend, or sister, if you weren't around. Well, just as well she'd found out before she'd done anything really stupid.

Only it already was too late—she had done something really stupid. She'd fallen in love with the two-timing rat and she was carrying his baby. At least she didn't have to compound these errors and move in with him.

Better to find out this way than come home one day to find him in bed with the au pair, she told herself, feeling so lucky she could have cried. In fact, she was crying; big, silent tears were rolling unheeded down her cheeks. Between Quinn and her hormones she'd cried more in the last forty-eight hours than she had in the previous four years—yet another reason to dump him. She never had understood women who stayed with a man who made them unhappy.

By the time Quinn caught up with her she had emerged from the broken, betrayed woman phase and progressed on to the icily controlled avenging goddess level—or maybe not…?

'Get out of my sight, you piece of slime!' she shrieked as he approached her smilingly. Anger, she told herself as a passing porter visibly recoiled, was an important part of the recovery process.

Quinn hastily rethought his plan—the one where he kissed her senseless. 'I think you scared that poor man.'

'*He* wasn't the target.'

'I sort of gathered that,' he responded mildly. 'Did you have a good journey, Rowena?'

'You weren't there,' she said, managing to imply this was a big plus point.

He still made no direct reference to her overt hostility, but his eyes had narrowed thoughtfully. 'Nothing's happened to your grandmother, has it?'

'No, she's fine.'

'I was worried when I found you'd left the hotel.' This was a masterly understatement; actually he'd been frantic. When he'd cooled down a bit, he'd apologised to the poor guy behind the bar for hurling a torrent of abuse and then half throttling him when he'd handed over the note Rowena had left for him.

'I can take care of myself.'

'I know that, but I enjoy taking care of you.'

If she hadn't known about his hypocrisy she'd have been putty in his hands after a line like that. Acknowledging her own weakness made her even angrier.

'I suppose you enjoy taking care of Holly too!' She laughed bitterly.

Quinn shook his head. 'You just lost me.'

'You do innocent confusion extremely well, but there's no point. I know *everything*!' she explained with a triumphant sneer.

'I had no idea you had a taste for high drama,' Quinn mused, starting to look slightly impatient.

'I know about you and Holly, how you slept with her in my bed, and don't try and deny it—she told me herself.'

'I doubt that very much.'

'Well, Niall might be crazy enough to forgive you, but not me! I'm glad he knocked you down—I hope it hurt.'

A reminiscent grin touched Quinn's lips as he ran his fingers along his angular jaw. 'It did.'

'I'm very *very* glad!' This malicious declaration was spoilt slightly by the great gulping sob that suddenly wracked her slender frame.

A decisive expression appeared on Quinn's face. 'This has gone on long enough!'

'What are you doing?' she asked as he suddenly grabbed her wrist in a firm manner. 'Let me go!' she demanded in a loud voice as he began to drag her forcibly down the corridor. 'I'll scream!'

Before she had time to put her threat into action Quinn stopped abruptly, read the sign on a door and pushed it open. A young man wearing a white coat sat dozing in one of the easy chairs with a newspaper propped up on his knee; he jerked upright as they walked in.

Quinn glanced at his name badge and nodded. 'We need some privacy,' he said, jerking his head towards the door.

'Right, yes, sir, of course.'

Rowena watched incredulously as he picked up his stethoscope and hurriedly left.

'Did he know you?' There was nothing about Quinn in his present garb to identify him as senior consultant.

Quinn shrugged. 'I don't think so.'

'Then I must be missing something—why did he go?'

Quinn shrugged. 'Because he knew we wanted to be alone?'

'Well, he was wrong. I don't want to be alone with you now or ever!'

'Well, that's too bad because you've no option.'

'What do you intend to do?' Rowena jeered, tossing her head. 'Lock me up?'

'No, marry you.'

This matter-of-fact statement robbed Rowena of her ability to think and articulate more than a muffled croak.

'But first I want to put you straight on a couple of things about that night at your flat. I'd heard you were home just for the weekend, I waited for you to call...but you didn't,' he recalled bleakly.

'I see, so it's *my* fault you jumped into bed with Holly.'

'I did not jump into bed with anyone. In fact,' he ground bitterly, 'I haven't even *noticed* another woman since you came back into my life! God, Rowena!' he groaned, grabbing her and drawing her roughly towards him. 'I'm so in love with you I haven't been able to think straight for months.'

He looked down into her wide, shocked eyes and gave a laugh of pure raw frustration.

'Why do you think I came to your flat that night?' he demanded. 'It wasn't to discuss the weather, woman! Like I said, I'd heard you were home. Of course, I didn't know you'd already scuttled back to New York by then. I stopped on the way over to take on board a little Dutch courage, but one thing led to another and I was blind drunk by the time I got there.' A spasm of weary distaste crossed his face. 'Pathetic, isn't it?'

'Being drunk is no excuse for sleeping with Holly…' she declared with a lot less certainty than earlier.

'For heaven's sake, woman,' Quinn ground out in the manner of a man clinging to the remnants of his control by the skin of his teeth. 'I haven't slept with Holly. The poor girl didn't have much choice but to let me take her bed for the night as I passed out cold. Then the next morning Niall turned up and thought much as you did… Actually, it was a relief to discover he and Holly were an item. At least that meant Niall was out of the picture…I've been wracked with jealousy about him.'

'Niall was never in the picture,' Rowena protested, shocked by the look of suffering that flickered darkly into his eyes. 'Why would he be?' she reflected bitterly. 'I don't love Niall,' she wailed, her voice rising steadily as her agitation increased. 'I *never* loved Niall, I've never loved anyone—not until you!' she finished breathlessly.

'Say that again!' he demanded, a light of fierce exhilaration shining in his deep-set eyes as they rested possessively on her upturned features.

Rowena shook her head. *'No way,'* she declared huskily. 'It was bad enough the first time.' She shot him a shy glance from under the sweep of her lashes. How could she have been scared of something that felt this gloriously good? she marvelled. *Quinn loved her*, he really did; she still couldn't believe it!

'You think it's a bad thing being in love with me?' he taunted tenderly.

'No, that's the problem.' She grabbed the lapels of his jacket and jerked him closer, her hungry eyes skimming over his dark, saturnine face. 'I think it's just about the best thing that has ever happened to me!' she declared passionately. 'Which only goes to prove, I've finally lost my mind.' And, boy, did it feel good! she thought as her heart beat out a wildly joyous tempo.

'Or maybe you've found it?'

'You could be right,' she admitted, emerging breathless from a long, lingering kiss.

'Personally, I prefer to think of love as a glorious sort of sanity in an otherwise crazy world.'

Rowena was enchanted by this unique slant.

He bent his head and took her waiting lips in a kiss so tender it brought tears to her eyes.

'I've been afraid of losing my…my… *identity*,' she said, struggling to explain her fears. 'I thought that was what being in love did to you, but it isn't like that, is it?' she appealed to him wonderingly. 'I feel more…'

'Complete?'

She gave a sigh of pleasure. 'I knew you'd understand.' Which is more than Holly would, she thought, belatedly recalling with horror the things she'd said to her sister. 'Oh, God!' she cried. 'If you didn't sleep with Holly…'

Quinn's face hardened. 'I thought we'd already dealt with that.'

Rowena pressed several very satisfactory sensual kisses to his lips to demonstrate her complete confidence in his innocence. Quinn kissed and touched her back—it was several minutes later before she was able to pick up the thread of her explanation.

'You don't understand, I said some really awful things to her. *Really* awful.'

'Don't worry. Holly has a soft spot for me, I'll talk her around.'

'Don't let Niall hear you saying that.' Rowena grinned. 'I wouldn't want him knocking you down again.'

'That only happened because I was in a *fragile* condition,' Quinn protested.

Rowena patted his arm. 'Of course it did, darling. Don't worry, I always did have a soft spot for a wimp,' she teased. Her expression suddenly sobered. 'When I came back from New York that weekend it was to see you,' she confessed huskily. 'I missed you so much…I kept thinking about what had happened. I wondered if there wasn't *some* way we could work things out. I even called your place once,' she confessed. 'And when I heard your voice I couldn't say *anything*. So I flew back to New York. I wish I'd been there that night when you arrived, not Holly.'

'I wasn't a pretty sight.'

'I think you're always a pretty sight.'

'Pretty, with this face…?' he mocked, pointing to his own dark countenance.

'All right, then, *beautiful*.' To her intense amusement Quinn looked embarrassed. 'About this marriage thing, Quinn…'

'You think it's too soon, you want a trial run? I can live with that…' It wouldn't be easy, but he had no choice. He needed Rowena.

'Maybe you can, but I don't think I can.'

A look of incredulity closely followed by fierce joy appeared on his face following her blunt declaration.

'But I need to know if you're only talking about marriage because of the baby?' Anxiously she scanned his face.

'The baby has nothing to do with it,' he told her forcefully. 'Don't get me wrong—I'm delighted about the idea of being a dad, but I wanted you for my wife a long time before I even knew there was going to be a baby.'

Rowena relaxed. 'In that case, hurry up and ask me,' she urged, tugging at his sleeve.

'I thought I already had.'

'No, you didn't ask me, you told me—a woman likes to be asked, but don't worry,' she added with a deliciously flirtatious smile. 'I'm going to say yes.'

It was funny, Quinn reflected, gazing adoringly into his future wife's eyes as he dropped down onto one knee, how one word could change a man's life for ever—he couldn't wait!

EPILOGUE

ROWENA took a quick peek in on the cassoulet before she returned to their guests. The good thing about rustic food, she reflected, picking up the tray of pre-dinner nibbles Quinn had rustled up while she got dressed, was that it didn't spoil, and in a household where the unexpected had a habit of cropping up at the last minute this was very useful.

The unexpected often involved their two-year-old son, Adam, who was meant to be asleep upstairs. The noises from the intercom as she returned to the drawing room made it quite clear that Adam was not asleep; it was equally clear that his poor father didn't have the faintest idea the intercom was switched on. Their guests had fallen silent as, with varying degrees of amusement, they listened to the distinguished surgeon's off-key rendering of 'One Man Went to Mow'.

'It's comforting to know Quinn isn't brilliant at *everything*,' one of his closest colleagues commented wryly as Rowena filled up his glass from one of the open bottles of wine on the coffee-table.

'I don't know,' his wife piped up. 'I think he sounds rather sweet.'

'If I ever needed any proof that you're tone deaf, darling…'

'That voice, I'll have you know,' Rowena told them sternly, 'is often the only thing that will send Adam to sleep. So when Quinn comes back down I don't want to hear any smart cracks—*Niall.*' She cast a pointed glance in her brother-in-law's direction.

'Now would I do that?' Niall replied, looking the picture of injured innocence.

Holly, curled up on the floor, lifted her head off his knee and prodded his thigh. She correctly detected the distinctive ring of insincerity in her husband's voice. 'Not if you know what's good for you,' she retorted sweetly.

With a tolerant smile Rowena watched this tart interchange. Despite what she had considered a mismatch of personalities, her sister's marriage seemed to still be in the honeymoon stage—she was happy for them.

'Sorry, folks.' She sighed apologetically. 'It looks like we'll be eating late again. Adam will not settle now until he's heard the chorus at least a dozen times.' Not wanting to inflict unnecessary suffering on their friends, she turned down the volume on the intercom to a low murmur before she lowered herself into a comfy seat.

She caught her sister's wondering glance and knew the way siblings sometimes do exactly what Holly was thinking. There were times when she too couldn't believe how much she'd changed over the past couple of years.

Once upon a time not producing a meal dead on time would have given her an anxiety attack, but these days she took such minor inconveniences calmly in her stride, the same way she didn't stress about the pile of unironed clothes waiting for the lady that *did* for them to come on Monday, and the broken catch on the kitchen garden gate that Quinn insisted he was quite capable of sorting—once he got the time.

With a sigh she slipped off her shoes and wriggled her toes. Her feet had been swelling during the last tiresome weeks of this pregnancy.

'Not long now,' Holly soothed sympathetically, pushing a footstool under Rowena's feet.

'Thank goodness!' Rowena breathed with a sigh. She patted her big belly affectionately. 'Hopefully this one will sleep through the night before he's eighteen months. At least there won't be the need for any boardroom breast-feeding this time,' she mused with a reminiscent smile.

This bold innovation had unsettled the senior management at the magazine almost as much as the crib in her office. After two boardroom sessions they'd suddenly developed a deep enthusiasm for the child-care facilities she'd been campaigning for—the very same plan they'd previously dumped on the grounds of financial unfeasibility!

But now, of course, Rowena didn't need the crèche. She was a successful author with a book that had landed straight in the best-seller lists both sides of the Atlantic and was still sitting there after six months.

'Who's going to play you in the film, Rowena?' Niall asked, shoving several stuffed olives in his mouth at one go. 'I hope Quinn isn't going to be too long, I haven't eaten since lunch.'

'You *pig*, Niall!' his wife reprimanded, smacking the hand stroking her neck with casual affection. 'And don't speak with your mouth full.'

'I think Gwyneth Paltrow, or maybe Michelle Pfeiffer would be a good choice,' mused her unrepentant mate. 'Though you're not as slim as you once were…'

With a grin Rowena patted her ample middle. 'Why, thank you, Niall, but actually I didn't retain casting rights. I just wrote the screenplay.' It was Quinn who had persuaded her she was more than up to the task.

'Just think, if Quinn hadn't sent your notebook to that publisher…?' Holly let the thought hang in the air.

Rowena nodded. She'd been furious at first with Quinn for sending to a publisher what she had considered her ramblings on the things that had happened to her during her pregnancy and the early mad months as a new mother. Her annoyance had turned to stunned amazement when they'd declared her ruminations one of the most original and amusing things they'd received in years.

As it turned out their confidence had been justified.

During a lull in the conversation the sound of Quinn's deep voice drifted around the room.

Rowena smiled to hear him say goodnight to their sleeping son.

''Night, champ, sleep tight.'

The love in his voice brought an emotional lump to Rowena's throat. She was just about to get up and dish up the meal when he continued.

'Hell, how did I get so lucky? You, my Rowena, and soon the baby…I suppose you do know you've got the best mother in the world? If this is a dream,' they all heard him reflect with husky sincerity, 'I hope I never wake up.'

Nobody said a word as Rowena moved over to the intercom and switched it off. She looked around at their guests.

'It was never on.'

'What was never on?' Niall responded with a wink and a mock puzzled frown.

'Thanks,' she gulped emotionally as she made a dash for the kitchen.

She sensed the moment Quinn entered the room.

'Is he asleep?'

'Finally,' Quinn said, coming up behind her and linking his arms around her middle. 'Do you think I'll ever be able to span your waist with my hands again?' he mused idly as he breathed in the sweet, familiar smell of her hair.

Love swelled like a bursting spring bud in her chest. 'Probably not.' She turned around and took his dear face between her hands and pressed her warm lips to his.

Several minutes later she drew back, her face flushed.

'What was that for?' Quinn asked, looking a bit hot himself.

'Just for being you,' she explained simply. 'Just for loving me and making me the happiest person alive. Is that a good enough reason?'

'Sounds good enough to me,' Quinn acknowledged, skilfully parting her lips with his tongue.

'Our guests are hungry!' she protested weakly.

'So am I!' Quinn growled.

Rowena, who had become pretty expert at prioritising, quickly decided which was more important—it helped when you were married to the best kisser in the world!

MILLS & BOON® PUBLISH EIGHT LARGE PRINT TITLES A MONTH. THESE ARE THE EIGHT TITLES FOR SEPTEMBER 2002

THE WEDDING ULTIMATUM
Helen Bianchin

HER BABY SECRET
Kim Lawrence

SWEET SURRENDER
Catherine George

LAZARO'S REVENGE
Jane Porter

HIS MAJESTY'S MARRIAGE
Winters & Gordon

THE CORPORATE BRIDEGROOM
Liz Fielding

THE TYCOON'S TEMPTATION
Renee Roszel

THEIR DOORSTEP BABY
Barbara Hannay

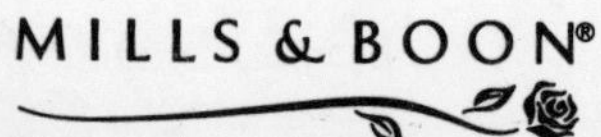

0802 Rom LP

MILLS & BOON® PUBLISH EIGHT LARGE PRINT TITLES A MONTH. THESE ARE THE EIGHT TITLES FOR OCTOBER 2002

THE ARRANGED MARRIAGE
Emma Darcy

THE DISOBEDIENT MISTRESS
Lynne Graham

THE GREEK TYCOON'S REVENGE
Jacqueline Baird

THE MARRIAGE PROPOSITION
Sara Craven

THE PRINCE'S PROPOSAL
Sophie Weston

THE MARRIAGE MERGER
Liz Fielding

THE BABY DILEMMA
Rebecca Winters

THE PREGNANCY PLAN
Grace Green